Dear Reader,

Once upon a time, I wrote a story that introduced a secondary character, Princess Julianna of Aliestle. I always thought she would be the perfect heroine to use in a Sleeping Beauty tale if the opportunity to write one ever presented itself.

In 2010, it finally did!

I was so excited to be asked to contribute to the *Once Upon a Kiss…* miniseries. I knew exactly what fairy tale I wanted to modernize and retell. When my editor told me I could do Sleeping Beauty, I actually squealed.

Of course, thinking about writing a contemporary fairy tale was easier than actually writing it. Not too many fairies and ogre queens around these days! I hope you'll see how I used elements from the classic tale as a springboard into this modern romance.

Princess Julianna has been sleepwalking through life far too long. It will take a special man—make that *prince*—to wake her up and make her see all that she is missing out on. A happily ever after is waiting for her if she'll just open her eyes and follow her heart!

Enjoy,

Melissa

MELISSA McCLONE

Not-So-Perfect Princess

TORONTO NEW YORK LONDON
AMSTERDAM PARIS SYDNEY HAMBURG
STOCKHOLM ATHENS TOKYO MILAN MADRID
PRAGUE WARSAW BUDAPEST AUCKLAND

Recycling programs
for this product may
not exist in your area.

ISBN-13: 978-0-373-74109-0

NOT-SO-PERFECT PRINCESS

First North American Publication 2011

Copyright © 2011 by Melissa Martinez McClone

This edition published by arrangement with Harlequin Books S.A.

For questions and comments about the quality of this book please contact us at Customer_eCare@Harlequin.ca.

www.Harlequin.com

Printed in U.S.A.

With a degree in mechanical engineering from Stanford University, the last thing **Melissa McClone** ever thought she would be doing was writing romance novels. But analyzing engines for a major U.S. airline just couldn't compete with her "happily-ever-afters." When she isn't writing, caring for her three young children or doing laundry, Melissa loves to curl up on the couch with a cup of tea, her cats and a good book. She enjoys watching home decorating shows to get ideas for her house—a 1939 cottage that is *slowly* being renovated. Melissa lives in Lake Oswego, Oregon, with her own real-life hero husband, two daughters, a son, two loveable but oh-so-spoiled indoor cats and a no-longer-stray outdoor kitty that decided to call the garage home. Melissa loves to her from her readers. You can write to her at P.O. Box 63, Lake Oswego, OR 97034, USA, or contact her via her website at www.melissamcclone.com.

For Tom

Special thanks to:
Elizabeth Boyle, Terri Reed,
Schmidt Chiropractic Center and the
Harlequin Romance team for letting me
tell Julianna's tale!

CHAPTER ONE

"THREE ARRANGED marriages and not one has made it to the altar. That is unacceptable!" King Alaric of Aliestle's voice thundered through the throne room like a lion's roar. Even the castle's tapestry-covered stone walls appeared to tremble. "If men think something is wrong with you, no amount of dowry will convince one to marry you."

Princess Julianna Louise Marie Von Schneckle didn't allow her father's harsh words to affect her posture. She stood erect with her shoulders back and her chin up, maximizing her five-foot-eight-inch-stature. The way she'd been taught to do by a bevy of governesses and nannies. Her stepmother didn't take a personal interest in her, but was diligent in ensuring she'd received the necessary training to be a perfect princess and queen.

"Father," Jules said evenly, not about to display an ounce of emotion. Tears and histrionics would play into her country's outdated gender stereotypes. They also wouldn't sway her father. "I was willing to marry Prince Niko, but he discovered Princess Isabel was alive and legally his wife. He had no choice but to end our arrangement."

Her father's nostrils flared. "The reason your match ended doesn't matter."

Jules understood why he was upset. He wanted to marry her off to a crown prince in order to put one of his grandchildren on a throne outside of Aliestle. He was willing to pay a king's ransom to make that happen. She'd become the wealthiest royal broodmare around. Unfortunately.

He glared down his patrician nose at her. "The result is the same. Three times now—"

"If I may, Father." Indignation made Jules speak up. She rarely interrupted her father. Okay, never. She was a dutiful daughter, but she wasn't going to take the blame for this. "You may have forgotten with all the other important matters on your mind, but you canceled my first match with Prince Christian. And Prince Richard was in love with an American when I arrived on San Montico."

"These failed engagements are still an embarrassment." Her father's frown deepened the lines on his face. The wrinkles reminded Jules of the valley crags in the Alps surrounding their small country. "A stain on our family name and Aliestle."

A lump of guilt lodged in her throat. Jules had been relieved when she found out Niko wouldn't be able to annul his first marriage and marry her. From the start, she'd hoped he would fall in love with his long-lost wife so Jules wouldn't have to get married.

Oh, she'd liked Vernonia with its loyal people and

lovely lakes for sailing. The handsome crown prince wanted to modernize his country, not be held back by antiquated customs. She would have had more freedom than she'd ever imagined as his wife and future queen. But she didn't love Niko.

Silly, given her country's tradition of arranged marriages. The realist in her knew the odds of marrying for love were slim to none, but the dream wouldn't die. It grew stronger with the end of each arranged match.

Too bad dreams didn't matter in Aliestle. Only duty.

Alaric shook his head. "If your mother were alive…"

Mother. Not stepmother.

Jules felt a pang in her heart. "If my mother were alive, I hope she would understand I tried my best."

She didn't remember her mother, Queen Brigitta, who had brought progressive, almost shocking, ideas to Aliestle when she married King Alaric. Though the match had been arranged, he fell so deeply in love with his young wife that he'd listened to her differing views on gender equality and proposed new laws at her urging, including higher education opportunities for women. He even took trips with her so she could indulge her passion for sailing despite vocal disapproval from the Council of Elders.

But after Brigitta died competing in a sailing race in the South Pacific when Jules was two, a heartbroken Alaric vowed never to go against convention again. He didn't rescind the legislation regarding education opportunities for women, but he placed limitations on the jobs females could hold and did nothing to improve their career prospects. He also remarried, taking as his wife and queen a proper Aliestlian noblewoman, one who knew her role and place in society.

"I'd hope my mother would see I've spent my life doing what was expected of me out of respect and love for you, my family and our country," Jules added.

But she knew a lifetime of pleasing others and doing good works didn't matter. Not in this patriarchal society where daughters, whether royal or commoner, were bartered like chattel. If Jules didn't marry and put at least one of her children on a throne somewhere, she would be considered a total failure. The obligation and pressure dragged Jules down like a steel anchor.

Her father narrowed his eyes. "I concede you're not to blame for the three matches ending. You've always been a good girl and obeyed my orders."

His words made her sound like a favored pet, not the beloved daughter he and her mother had spent ten years trying to conceive. Jules wasn't surprised. Women were treated no differently than lapdogs in Aliestle.

Of course, she'd done nothing to dispel the image. She was as guilty as her father and the Council of Elders for allowing the stereotyping and treatment of women to continue. As a child, she'd learned Aliestle didn't want her to be as independent and outspoken as her mother had been. They wanted Jules to be exactly what she was—a dutiful princess who didn't rock the boat. But she hoped to change that once she married and lived outside of Aliestle. She would then be free to help her brother Brandt, the crown prince, so he could modernize their country and improve women's rights when he became king.

Her father eyed her speculatively. "I suppose it would be premature to marry you off to the heir of an Elder."

A protest formed in the back of her throat, but Jules pressed her lips together to keep from speaking out. She'd said more than she intended. She had to maintain a cool and calm image even if her insides trembled.

Marrying a royal from Aliestle would keep her stuck in this repressive country forever. Her children, most especially daughters, would face the same obstacles she faced now.

Jules fought a rising panic. "Please, Father, give me another chance. The next match will be successful. I'll do whatever it takes to marry."

He raised a brow. "Such enthusiasm."

More like desperation. She forced the corners of her mouth into a practiced smile. "Well, I'm twenty-eight, father. My biological clock is ticking."

"Ah, grandchildren." He beamed, as if another rare natural resource had been discovered in the mountains of Aliestle. "They are the only thing missing in my life. I shall secure you a fourth match right away. Given your track record, I had a backup candidate in mind when you left for Vernonia."

A backup? His lack of confidence stabbed at her heart.

"All I need to do is negotiate the marriage contract," he continued.

That would take about five minutes given her dowry.

"Who am I to marry, Father?" Jules asked, as if she wanted to know the person joining them for dinner, not the man she would spend the rest of her life with in a loveless marriage negotiated for the benefit of two countries. But anyone would be better than marrying an Aliestlian.

"Crown Prince Enrique of La Isla de la Aurora."

"The Island of the Dawn," she translated.

"It's a small island in the Mediterranean off the coast of Spain ruled by King Dario."

Memories of San Montico, another island in the Mediterranean where Crown Prince Richard de Thierry ruled, surfaced. All citizens had equal rights. Arranged marriages were rare though the country had a few old-fashioned customs. She hadn't been allowed to sail there, but the water and wind had been perfect.

Longing stirred deep inside Jules.

Sailing was her inheritance from her mother and the one place she felt connected to the woman she didn't remember. It was the only thing Jules did for herself. No matter what life handed out, no matter what tradition she was forced to abide by, she could escape her fate for a few hours when she was on the water.

But only on lakes and rivers.

After Jules learned to sail on the Black Sea while visiting her maternal grandparents, her father had forbidden her to sail on the ocean out of fear she would suffer the same fate as her mother. Two decades later, he still treated Jules like a little girl. Perhaps now he would finally see her as an adult, even though she was female, and change his mind about the restrictions.

"Am I allowed to sail when I'm on the island?" she asked.

"Sailing on the sea is forbidden during your engagement."

Hope blossomed at his words. He'd never left her an opening before. "After I'm married…?"

"Your husband can decide the fate of your… hobby."

Not hobby. Passion.

When she was on a boat, only the moment mattered. The wind against her face. The salt in the air. The tiller or a sheet in her hand. She could forget she was Her Royal Highness Princess Julianna and be Jules. Nothing but sailing had ever made her feel so…free.

If La Isla de la Aurora were a progressive island like San Montico, she would have freedom, choice and be allowed to sail on the ocean. Her heart swelled with anticipation. That would be enough to make up for not marrying for love.

"Understand, Julianna, this is your final match outside of Aliestle," he said firmly. "If Prince Enrique decides he doesn't want to marry you, you'll marry one of the Elder's heirs upon your return home."

A shiver shot down her spine. "I understand, Father."

"You may want to push for a short engagement," he added.

A very short one.

Jules couldn't afford to have Prince Enrique change his mind about marrying her. She had to convince him she was the only woman for him. The perfect princess for him. And maybe she would find the love she dreamed about on the island. Her parents had fallen in love through an arranged marriage. It could happen to her, too.

She'd avoided thinking about tomorrow. Now she looked forward to the future. "When do I leave for the island, sir?"

"If I complete negotiations with King Dario and Prince Enrique tonight, you may leave tomorrow." Alaric said. "Your brother Brandt, a maid and a body-guard will accompany you."

This was Jules's last chance for a life of freedom. Not only for herself, but her children and her country. She couldn't make any mistakes. "I'll be ready to depart in the morning, Father."

Lying in bed, Alejandro Cierzo de Amanecer heard a noise outside his room at the beachfront villa. The stray kitten he'd found at the boatyard must want something. He opened his eyes to see sunlight streaming in through the brand-new floor-to-ceiling windows. Most likely breakfast.

The bedroom door burst wide-open. Heavy boots sounded against the recently replaced terra-cotta tile floor.

Not again.

Alejandro grimaced, but didn't move. He knew the routine.

A squad of royal guards dressed in blue and gold uniforms surrounded his bed. At least they hadn't drawn their weapons this time. Not that he would call another intrusion progress.

"What does *he* want now?" Alejandro asked.

The captain of the guard, Sergio Mendoza, looked as stoic as ever, but older with gray hair at his temples. "King Dario requests your presence at the palace, Your Highness."

Alejandro raked his hand through his hair in frustration. "My father never requests anything."

Sergio's facial expression didn't change. He'd only shown emotion once, when Alejandro had been late bringing Sergio's youngest daughter home from a date when they were teenagers. In spite of the security detail accompanying them, Alejandro had feared for his life due to the anger in the captain's eyes.

"The king orders you to come with us now, sir," Sergio said.

Alejandro didn't understand why his father wanted to see him. No one at the palace listened to what Alejandro said. He might not want to be part of the monarchy, but he wasn't about to abandon his country.

He'd founded his business here and suggested economic innovations, including developing their tourist trade. But his ideas clashed with those of his father and brother who were more old-fashioned and traditional in their thinking.

A high-pitched squeak sounded. The scraggly black kitten with four white paws clawed his way up the sheet onto the bed. The thing had been a nuisance these past two weeks with the work at the boatyard and renovations here at the villa.

"I need to get dressed before I go anywhere," Alejandro said.

"We'll wait while you dress, sir." Sergio's words did nothing to loosen Alejandro's tense shoulder muscles. "The king wants no delay in your arrival."

Alejandro clenched his teeth. He wanted to tell the loyal captain to leave, but the guards would use force to get him to do what they wanted. He was tired of fighting that battle. "I need privacy."

Sergio ordered the soldiers out of the room, but he remained standing by the bed. "I'll wait on the other side of the door, sir. Guards are stationed beneath each window."

Alejandro rolled his eyes. His father still saw him as a rebellious teenager. "I'm thirty years old, not seventeen."

Sergio didn't say anything. No doubt the captain remembered some of Alejandro's earlier…escapades.

"Tell me where you think I would run to, Captain?"

Alejandro lay in bed covered with a sheet. "My business is here. I own properties. My father's lackeys follow me wherever I go."

"They are your security detail, sir," Sergio said. "You must be protected. You're the second in line for the throne."

"Don't remind me," Alejandro muttered.

"Many would give everything to be in your position."

Not if they knew what being the "spare" entailed. No one cared what he thought. Even when he tried to help the island, no one supported him. He'd had to do everything on his own.

Alejandro hated being a prince. He'd been educated in the United States. He didn't want to participate in an outdated form of government where too much power rested with one individual. But he wanted to see his country prosper.

"Guard the door if you must." Alejandro gave the kitten a pat. "I won't make your job any more difficult for you than it is."

As soon as Sergio left, Alejandro slid out of bed and showered. His father hadn't requested formal dress so khaki shorts, a navy T-shirt and a pair of boat shoes would do.

Twenty minutes later, Alejandro entered the palace's reception room. His older brother rose from the damask-covered settee. Enrique looked like a younger version of their father with his short hairstyle, tailored designer suit, starched dress shirt, silk tie and polished leather shoes. It was too bad his brother acted like their father, also.

"This had better be important, Enrique," Alejandro said.

"It is." His brother's lips curved into a smug smile. "I'm getting married."

About time. Enrique's wedding would be the first step toward Alejandro's freedom from the monarchy. The birth of a nephew or niece to take his place as second in line for the throne would be the next big step. "Congratulations, bro. I hope it's a short engagement. Don't waste any time getting your bride pregnant."

Enrique smirked. "That's the plan."

"Why wait until the wedding? Start now."

He laughed. "King Alaric would demand my head if I did that. He's old-fashioned about certain things. Especially his daughter's virginity."

"Alaric." Alejandro had heard the name. It took a second to realize where. "You're marrying a princess from Aliestle?"

"Not a princess. *The* princess." Enrique sounded excited. No wonder. Aliestle was a small kingdom in the Alps. With an abundance of natural resources, the country's treasury was vast, a hundred times that of La Isla de la Aurora. "King Alaric has four sons and one daughter."

"Father must be pleased."

"He's giddy over the amount of Julianna's dowry and the economic advantages aligning with Aliestle will bring us. Fortunately for me, the princess is as beautiful as she is rich. A bit of an ice princess from what I hear, but I'll warm her up."

"If you need lessons—"

"I may not have your reputation with the ladies, but I shall manage fine on my own."

"I hope the two of you are happy together." Alejandro meant the words. A happy union would mean more heirs. The further Alejandro dropped in the line of succession, the better. He couldn't wait to be able to focus his attention on building his business and attracting more investors to turn the island's sluggish economy around.

"You are to be the best man."

A statement of fact or a request? "Mingling with aristocracy is hazardous to my health."

"You will move home until the wedding."

A demand. Anger flared. "Enrique—"

"The royal family will show a united front during the engagement period. Your days will be free unless official events are scheduled. You'll be expected to attend all dinners and evening functions. You must also be present when the princess and her party arrive today."

Alejandro cursed. "You sound exactly like him."

"They are Father's words, not mine." Rare compassion filled Enrique's eyes. "But I would like you to be my best man. You're my favorite brother."

"I'm your only brother."

Enrique laughed. "All the more reason for you to

stand at my side. Father will compensate you for any inconvenience."

Alejandro's entire life was a damn inconvenience. Besides, he would never be able to get the one thing he wanted from his father. "I don't want *his* money."

"You never have, but when Father offers you payment, take it. You can put the money into your boats, buy another villa, donate it to charity or give it away on the streets," Enrique advised. "You've earned this, Alejandro. Don't let pride get in the way again."

He wasn't about to go there. "All I want is to be left alone."

"As soon as Julianna and I have children, you will no longer be needed around here. If you do your part to ensure the wedding occurs, Father has promised to let you live your own life."

Finally. "Did you ask for this or did Father offer?"

"It was a combination, but be assured of Father keeping his word."

"When am I to move back?"

"After lunch."

Alejandro cursed again. He had a boatyard to run, investment properties to oversee and the Med Cup to prepare for. Not to mention the kitten who expected to be fed. "I have a life. Responsibilities."

"You have responsibilities here. Ones you ignore while you play with your boats," Enrique chided.

Seething, Alejandro tried to keep his tone even. "I'm not playing. I'm working. If you'd see the upcoming Med Cup race as an opportunity to promote—"

"If you want to build the island's reputation, then

support this royal wedding. It'll do much more for the economy than your expensive ideas to improve the island's nightlife, build flashy resorts and attract the sailing crowd with a little regatta."

"The Med Cup is a big deal. It'll—"

"Whatever." Enrique brushed Alejandro aside as if he were a bothersome gnat. Like father, like son. "Do what you must to be here after lunch or Father will send you away on a diplomatic mission."

The words were like a punch to Alejandro's solar plexus. Not unexpected given the way his father and brother operated sometimes. The threat would be carried out, too. That meant Alejandro had to do as told to secure his future. His freedom.

"I'll be back before your princess arrives."

But he would be doing a few things his way.

Once the black sheep, always the black sheep.

And let's face it, Alejandro didn't mind the title at all.

A helicopter whisked Jules over the clear, blue Mediterranean Sea. The luxurious cabin with large, leather seats comfortably fit the four of them: her, Brandt, Yvette her maid and Klaus their bodyguard. But even with soundproofing, each wore headsets to communicate and protect their ears from the noise of the rotors.

Almost there.

A combination of excitement and nerves made Jules want to tap her toes and twist the ends of her hair with her finger. She kept her hands clasped on her lap instead. She wanted to make her family and country proud. Her mother, God rest her soul, too. Presenting the image of a princess completely in control was important, even if doing so wasn't always easy.

She glanced out the window. Below, on the water, a Sun Fast 3200 with a colorful spinnaker caught her eye. She pressed her forehead against the window to get a better look at the sailboat.

Gorgeous.

The crew sat on the rail, their legs dangling over the side. The hull planed across the waves.

Longing made it difficult to breath.

What she wouldn't give to be on that boat sailing away from the island instead of flying toward the stranger who would be her husband and the father of her children... But she shouldn't wish that. Jules had a responsibility, a duty, the same that had been thrust upon her mother so many years ago. Marrying Prince Enrique had to be better than being stuck in patriarchal Aliestle for the rest of her life. At least, she hoped so. If not...

Jules grimaced.

"You okay?" Brandt's voice asked through her headset.

She shrugged. "I think I'm cursed. When my godparents offered gifts at my christening, one of them must have cursed me to a life of duty with no reward. A loveless arranged marriage."

And an unfulfilled yearning for adventure and freedom.

"Look out the window," Brandt said. "You're not cursed, Jules. You're going to be living on a vacation paradise."

Crescents of postcard-worthy white sand beaches came into view. Palm trees seemed to stand at attention, except for the few arching toward the ground. The beach gave way to a town. Pastel-colored, tiled roofed buildings and narrow streets dotted the hillsides above the village center.

She glimpsed rows of sailboats moored at a marina. The masts, tall and shiny, rocked starboard and port like metronomes. Her mouth went dry.

Perhaps cursed was the wrong word. All these sailboats had to be a good sign, right? "Maybe life will be different here."

"It will." Brandt smiled, the same charming smile she'd seen on a cover of a tabloid at the airport in Spain. "Your fiancé will be unable to resist your beauty and intelligence. He'll fall head over heels in love with you and allow you to do whatever you wish. Including sailing on the ocean."

She wiggled her toes in anticipation. "I hope that's true."

"Believe," he encouraged. "That's what you always tell me."

Yes, she did. But this situation was different. Jules knew nothing about Prince Enrique. She'd been so busy preparing for her departure she hadn't had time to look him up on the internet. Not that she had a choice in marrying him even if he turned out to be an ogre.

For all she knew he was old with one foot in the grave. Okay, now she was overreacting. Her father had always matched her with younger men because he wanted grandchildren. This match shouldn't be any different.

Jules hoped Enrique was charming, handsome and would sweep her off her feet. She wanted to find him attractive and be able to love him. She also wanted his heart to be free and open to loving her in return.

Her concern ratcheted. Prince Richard and Prince Niko had been in love with other women. If Enrique's affections were attached to a girlfriend or mistress that wouldn't bode well for their match reaching the altar or, if it did, love developing between them.

Jules shifted in her seat. "I do hope this island has up-to-date ideas about women."

"It has to be more contemporary. Aliestle has been asleep since the Middle Ages." Brandt cupped one side of his headset with his hand. "Listen, I hear Father snoring now. The tyrant could wake the dead."

A smile tugged at the corners of Jules's mouth. "Too bad we can't wake him."

"Along with the entire Council of Elders."

Nodding, she stared at her brother who was more known as a playboy crown prince than a burgeoning politician and ruler. "When you're king, you'll change the way things are done."

Brandt shrugged. "Being king will be too much work."

"You'll rise to the occasion," she encouraged.

He gave her a look. "You really think so?"

"Yes." Her gaze locked with his, willing him to remember their previous discussions and their plan. Okay, her plan. "You will bring our country into the twenty-first century. If not for our younger brothers and subjects, then for your children and theirs. Especially the daughters."

"I don't know."

"Yes, you do. And I'll help." The bane of his existence was being crown prince. Brandt wanted all the perks that went with being royalty without any of the responsibility. One of these days he was going to have to grow up. "Once I marry someone outside of Aliestle, Father's reign over me ends. I'll be able to represent our country to the world and gain support to help you enact reforms when you are king, even if the Council of Elders is against them. We must change Aliestle for the better, Brandt."

He didn't say anything. She didn't expect him to.

"We are approaching the palace," the pilot announced over the headsets.

Goose bumps prickled Jules's skin.

Full of curiosity at her new home, she peered out the window. A huge white stucco and orange-tile roofed palace perched above the sea. The multistoried building had numerous balconies and windows.

But no tower. Another good sign?

A paved road and narrower walking paths wove their way through a landscape of palm trees, flowering bushes and manicured greenery. Water shot at least twenty-five feet into the air from an ornately decorated fountain.

The Mediterranean island and palace were a world away from Aliestle and the stone castle fortress nestled high in the Alps. Living somewhere lighter and brighter would be a welcome change from the Grimm-like fairy-tale setting she called home.

"Father may have finally gotten this right," Brandt said.

Jules nodded. "It's pretty."

"At least on the outside."

She sighed. "Don't forget, dear brother, you're here for moral support."

"And to make sure the honeymoon doesn't start early," Brandt joked.

As if she'd ever had that opportunity present itself. She glared at him. "Be quiet."

"Sore spot, huh?"

He had no idea. Engaged three times, and she'd never come close to anything other than kisses. Besides making out with Christian while a teenager, she'd been kissed once as an adult. Prince Niko's kiss while sailing had been pleasant enough, but nothing like the passion she'd overheard other women discussing. Perhaps with Prince Enrique…

The helicopter landed on a helipad. The engine stopped. The rotor's rotation slowed. Her hand trembled, making her work harder to unbuckle her harness. Finally she undid the latch. As they exited, a uniformed staff member placed their luggage onto a wheeled cart.

"Welcome to La Isla de la Aurora, Your Royal Highness Crown Prince Brandt and Your Royal

Highness Princess Julianna." An older man in a gray suit bowed. "I am Ortiz. Prince Enrique sends his regrets for not meeting you himself, but he is attending to important state business at the moment."

"We understand." Brandt smiled. He might not be the typical statesman, but no one could fault his friendliness. "State business comes first."

Jules looked around at the potted plants and flowering vines. A floral scent lingered in the air. Paradise? Perhaps.

"Thank you, sir." Ortiz sounded grateful. "I am in charge of the palace and at your service. Whatever you need, I'll see that you have it."

Jules glanced at Brandt, whose grin resembled the Cheshire cat's. She would have to make sure he didn't take advantage of the generous offer of hospitality.

"The palace grounds are lovely, Ortiz," she said. "Very inviting with so many colorful flowers and plants."

"I am happy you like it, ma'am." His smile took years off his tanned, lined face. "Please allow me to show you and your party inside."

Klaus nodded. Her bodyguard, in his fifties with a crew cut and a gun hidden under his tailored suit jacket, had protected her for as long as she could remember.

"Lead the way, Ortiz," she said.

As they walked from the helipad to the front door, Ortiz gave her a brief history lesson about the palace. She had no idea the royal family had ruled the island for so long. No doubt the continuous line of succession had impressed her father who would want to ensure a long reign for his grandchildren and the heirs that followed.

"Prince Enrique has done so much for the island," Ortiz said. "A finer successor to King Dario cannot be found, ma'am."

If only Jules knew whether the compliments were truthful or propaganda. She knew little about her future husband besides his name. "I'm looking forward to meeting Prince Enrique."

Ortiz beamed. "He said the same thing about you at lunchtime, ma'am."

A third good sign? Jules hoped so.

When they reached the palace entry, two arched wooden doors parted as if by magic. Once the heavy doors were fully open, she saw two uniformed attendants standing behind and holding them.

Jules stared at the entrance with a mix of anticipation and apprehension. If all went well—and she hoped it did—this palace would be her new home. She would live with her husband and raise her children here. She fought the urge to cross her fingers.

With a deep breath, she stepped inside. The others followed.

A thirty-foot ceiling gave the large marble tiled foyer an open and airy feel. Stunning paintings, a mix of modern and classical works, hung on the walls. A marble statue of a woman sitting in the middle captured Jules's attention. "What an amazing sculpture."

"That is Eos, one of the Greek's second generation

Titan gods," Ortiz explained. "We are more partial to the Latin name, Aurora. Whichever name you prefer, she'll always be the Goddess of the Dawn."

"Beautiful," Brandt agreed. "Eos had a strong desire for handsome young men. If she looked anything like this statue, I'm sure she had no trouble finding willing lovers."

"Close the front doors," a male voice shouted. "Now."

The attendants pushed the heavy doors. Grunts sounded. Muscles strained.

"Hurry," the voice urged.

The people behind Jules rushed farther into the foyer so the doors could be shut. The momentum pushed her forward.

A shirtless man wearing shorts ran toward the doors. Something black darted across the floor.

Yvette screamed. "A rat, Your Highnesses."

"There are no rats in the palace," Ortiz shouted.

The ball of black fur darted between Jules's legs. Startled, she stumbled face-first.

"Catch her," Klaus yelled.

Too late. The marble floor seemed to rise up to meet Jules though she was the one falling.

She stopped abruptly. Not against the floor.

Strong arms embraced Jules. Her face pressed against a hard, bare chest. Her cheek rested against warm skin. Dark hair tickled her nose. The sound of a heartbeat filled her ears. He smelled so good. No fancy colognes. Only soap and water and salty ocean air.

She wanted another sniff.

Ortiz shrieked. "Your Highnesses. Are either of you hurt?"

Highnesses? The man must be a prince. Her father had only spoken of the crown prince. No other brothers had been mentioned. Oh, if this were Enrique...

CHAPTER TWO

"JULES?" BRANDT sounded concerned.

"I'm fine," Jules said quickly, more interested in the man—the prince—who saved her from hitting her face on the floor and still held her with his strong arms. Such wide shoulders, too.

Awareness seeped through her.

"My apologies." His deep, rich voice and Spanish accent sent her racing pulse into a mad sprint. "The kitten darted out of the room before I could grab him."

Ortiz raised his chin. "As I said, there are no rats in the palace, Princess."

The prince inhaled sharply. She found herself being set upon her feet. But he kept hold of her, even after she was standing.

"Stable?" he asked.

She nodded, forcing herself not to stare at his muscular chest and ripped abs.

He let go of her.

A chill shivered through Jules. She wasn't used to being in such close contact with anyone, but she missed having his nicely muscled arms around her.

She studied him, eager for a better look.

Over six feet tall with an athletic build, he looked more pirate than prince with shoulder-length dark brown hair, an earring in his left ear, khaki shorts and bare feet.

His strong jawline, high cheekbones and straight nose looked almost chiseled and made her think of the Eos sculpture. But his full lips and thick eyelashes softened the harsher features. The result—a gorgeous face she would be happy to stare at for hours. Days. Years.

Jules's heart thudded. "Thank you."

Warm brown eyes met hers. Gold specks flickered like flames around his irises. "You're welcome."

Everyone else faded into the background. Time seemed to stop. Something unfamiliar unfurled deep inside her.

He swooped up a black ball of fur with one hand. The look of tenderness in his dark eyes as he checked the kitten melted her heart. She would love for a man—this man—to look at her that way.

The kitten meowed. As he rubbed it, he returned his attention to her. "You're Princess Julianna from Aliestle."

It wasn't a question.

"Yes." Jules had never believed in love at first sight until now. She hoped their children looked exactly like him. A smile spread across her lips and reached all the way to her heart. Her father *had* gotten this right. She would realize her dream of marrying for love. A warm glow flowed through her. "You must be Enrique."

"No." His jaw thrust forward. "I am Alejandro."

Alejandro held on to the kitten as confusion clouded Juliana's pretty face. He was a little confused by his own reaction to this so-called ice princess. She had practically melted against him, and he'd yet to cool down from the contact. The woman was gorgeous, with a killer body underneath her coral-colored suit, long blond hair and big blue eyes a man could drown in.

She smelled sweet, like a bouquet of wildflowers. He wondered if her glossed lips tasted...

Not sweet.

He forced his gaze off her mouth. Julianna's marriage to Enrique and the children she conceived would remove Alejandro from the line of succession. She was his ticket out of his obligation to the monarchy. He couldn't think of her as anything other than his future sister-in-law.

That shouldn't be difficult since she wasn't his type.

Beautiful, yes, if you liked the kind of woman who knew how to apply makeup perfectly and could give any supermodel a run for her money. But he wanted a woman who didn't care about the trappings of wealth and royalty. A woman who was down-to-earth and didn't mind the spray of salt water in her face.

"Alejandro," Julianna repeated as if he didn't know his own name.

He couldn't remember the last time anyone had mistaken him for Enrique. Polar opposites didn't begin to describe their differences. But the fact Julianna didn't know what her future husband looked like surprised Alejandro more. Arranged marriages were still a part of royal life in some countries, but agreeing to marry someone without seeing their photograph struck him as odd. "Yes."

She stiffened. The warmth in her eyes disappeared. The expression on her face turned downright chilly.

Ice princess?

He saw now why she'd been called that. The change in her demeanor startled him, but he shouldn't have been surprised. Alejandro had dated enough spoiled and pampered royals and wealthy girls to last a lifetime. This one, with a rich-as-Midas father, would most likely rank up there with the worst. He almost pitied Enrique. Emphasis on almost.

She drew her finely arched brows together, looking haughty not curious. "That makes you...?"

The kitten chirped, sounding more bird than cat. Alejandro used his thumb to rub under the cat's chin.

Impatience flashed in Julianna's eyes.

He took his time answering. "Enrique's younger brother."

Alejandro waited for her look of disdain. No one cared about the second in line for the throne, especially a woman meant to be queen.

"Oh." Her face remained expressionless. But royals were trained to turn off emotion with the flick of a switch and not display their true feelings. "I didn't realize Enrique had a younger brother."

That Alejandro believed. "My family prefers not to talk about me."

Ortiz cleared his throat.

"The princess will be family soon enough, Ortiz." Alejandro would be counting the days as soon as the official wedding date was set. He couldn't wait to live his own life without interference from his family. Of course, an heir or two would need to be born until he would be totally free. He shifted his gaze to the princess. "She'll hear the stories. Whispers over tea. Innuendos over cocktails. Nudges during dessert. No sense hiding the truth."

Tilting her chin, she gave him a cool look. "What truth might that be?"

"I'm the black sheep of the family."

Julianna pursed her lips. "A black cat for the black sheep."

"Not by choice," he admitted. "The cat chose me."

She stared at the kitten, but didn't pet him. Definitely ice running through her veins. "Such a lucky kitty to be able to choose for itself."

"It's too bad royalty doesn't get the same choices," Alejandro said.

He waited for her to reply. She didn't.

"Eat, sleep, play." A man in his early twenties with dark, curly brown hair stepped forward. He had rugged features, but his refined demeanor matched his designer suit and Italian leather shoes. "The life of a cat seems perfect to me. Much better than that of a prince."

"Well, the kitten is a stray," Alejandro said. "Caviar isn't part of his diet."

The man grinned. "It's only part of mine on occasion."

Julianna sighed. "Prince Alejandro, this is—"

"Alejandro," he corrected. "I don't use my title."

"Wish I could get away with that," the other man said. "Though the title does come in handy when it comes to women."

"That is the one benefit I have found," Alejandro agreed.

Julianna rolled her eyes. "The two of you can compare dating notes later. Now it's time for a formal introduction."

The princess's words told Alejandro she was cut from the same cloth as Enrique. Both seemed to hold an appreciation for royal protocol and etiquette. Something Alejandro saw as a complete waste of time. The two stuffy royals might live happily ever after.

"Alejandro," she continued. "This is His Royal Highness Crown Prince Brandt. One of my four younger brothers."

Brother? Alejandro studied the two. He couldn't believe they were so closely related. Brandt was as dark as his sister was fair.

"Half brother," Julianna clarified, as if reading Alejandro's thoughts.

That explained it. But nothing explained why his

gaze drifted to the curve of her hips. A nice body would never make up for an unpleasant personality that was the female version of his older brother. Maybe he'd been spending too much time working at the boatyard and not enough time out partying with the ladies. Perhaps later...

Right now he wanted to return to his room. Being surrounded by royalty was suffocating.

"It's been nice meeting you." His obligation to be here when the princess arrived had been met. He cradled the now napping kitten in the crook of his arm. "I'll see..."

Julianna stroked the kitten. The move took him by surprise. The soft smile on her face reached all the way to her eyes and made him do a double-take. His pulse rate shot up a few notches.

He'd always been a sucker for a pair of big baby blues. "Would you like to hold him?"

She drew back her hand. Her French manicured nails had no cracks or chips. "No, thank you."

Alejandro didn't know whether to be intrigued or annoyed by the princess. Before he could decide which, a cloud of strong aftershave hit him. He recognized the toxic scent, otherwise known as the expensive designer brand of cologne his brother wore.

Enrique turned the corner. He strode across the floor with quick steps and his head held high. Whereas Brandt looked regal, Enrique came across as pompous.

He stared at Julianna as if she were a red diamond, a rare gem meant only for him. Dollar signs shone in his eyes. Enrique's priority had always been La Isla de la Aurora. Women were secondary, which was why an arranged marriage had been necessary.

After an uncomfortable moment of silence, Enrique glared at Ortiz, who introduced everyone with lofty titles and more middle names than Alejandro could count.

Enrique struck a ridiculous pose, as if he were at a photo shoot not standing in the foyer. "I hope you had a pleasant journey from Aliestle."

"Thank you. I did." Julianna's polite smile gave nothing away as to her first impression of her groom. "The palace is lovely."

Leave it to Enrique to turn meeting his future wife into such a formal event. Alejandro couldn't believe his brother. Didn't he remember their charm lessons with Mrs. Delgado? If Enrique had a clue about women, about Julianna, he would kiss her hand and compliment her on her shoes. He would make her feel as if she'd arrived home, not treat her like a temporary houseguest. But Enrique only did what he wanted, no matter how that affected anyone else.

"Alejandro." Irritation filled Enrique's eyes. "What are you doing with that animal?"

"He's a kitten. And I'm only following your instructions, brother," Alejandro explained. "I'm here, as requested, to meet your lovely bride."

Enrique's face reddened. "You could at least have taken the time to dress."

"He escaped while I was changing." Alejandro petted

the sleeping cat. "I assumed Father wouldn't want a kitten tearing through the palace unattended."

Enrique started to speak then stopped himself. Their guests must be keeping his temper in check. At least the princess and her entourage were good for something around here.

"I'll take him to my room," Alejandro added. "See you at dinner."

"Formal attire," Enrique reminded, his voice tight. "In case you've forgotten, that includes shirt and shoes."

Alejandro rocked back on his heels. "I know how to dress for dinner, bro, but thanks for the reminder."

The air crackled with tension.

Twenty years ago, they would have been fighting while Ortiz called for the palace guards to separate them. Ten years ago, the same thing might have happened. But Enrique would never lower himself, or his station, to that level now. Even if his hard gaze told Alejandro he wanted to fight.

"At least your younger brother knows how to dress, Enrique. Not all of mine do." Julianna sounded empathetic. "I don't know about you, but sometimes it's hard being the oldest."

Her words may have been calculated, but they did the trick. Enrique's jaw relaxed. He focused his attention on Julianna.

Alejandro was impressed. Diffusing the situation so deftly took skill. And practice.

"It can be difficult." The corners of Enrique's mouth lifted into a half smile. "Younger siblings don't take things as seriously or have the same sense of duty."

Idiot. Alejandro wondered if his brother realized he was also slamming Brandt, another crown prince, with his words.

"Some don't," Julianna agreed. "But others just need to understand their responsibilities a little better. Isn't that right, dear brother?"

Brandt nodded, looking more amused than offended. Alejandro liked the guy already.

Enrique's mouth twisted, as if he finally understood how his words could be construed. "I was talking about Alejandro."

Julianna smiled at Enrique. "Of course, you were."

The woman was smooth. Alejandro had no idea if her skills came from dealing with her brothers or boyfriends, but he'd never seen anyone handle Enrique so well. Not even their mother who had separated from their father years ago. Maybe Julianna could rein in the future ruler's ego and temper. If she had a brain in that pretty head of hers, as she seemed to, she could stop him from making bad decisions, like focusing on projects that aggrandized himself, but did nothing to help the island.

The ice princess might be exactly what Enrique needed.

Alejandro would have to make sure his brother didn't blow this engagement.

For both their sakes. And the island's.

* * *

"Thank you for escorting me to my room." Standing with Enrique, Jules glanced around. The pastel pink and yellow decor was bright and cheery. Maybe some of it would rub off on her because right now she was feeling a little...down. She forced a smile anyway. Replacing Enrique's aftershave and teaching him a few manners wouldn't be difficult. It could be much worse. "The suite is lovely."

"I asked Ortiz to put you in this room." Enrique pulled back a curtain. "I thought you might like the view."

She stared out the window at rows of colorful flowers below. A burst of hot pink. A swatch of bright yellow. A patch of purple.

Another wave of disappointment washed over her. The same way it had when she'd discovered her hottie rescuer wasn't going to be her husband, but her brother-in-law.

Don't think about that. About him. Otherwise she might find herself back in Aliestle.

"A garden." She hoped she sounded more enthusiastic than she felt. A bush of red roses captured her attention until she noticed the large thorns on the thick stems. Ouch, that would hurt. "How nice."

"The garden is the closest thing I have to a hobby now. A majority of the flowers are in bloom," Enrique explained. "When you open the window, the breeze will carry a light floral scent into your room."

"Picking out this room for me is so thoughtful of you." Even if she would have preferred the smell of salt water, a view of the sea, Alejandro.

No, that wasn't fair.

Enrique was handsome. He looked more like a fashion model from Milan than a crown prince in his designer suit, starched shirt, silk tie and leather shoes. If he'd been shirtless and she found herself pressed against his hard chest...

She tried to imagine it. Tried and failed.

He wasn't Alejandro, who had appeared in the foyer like the Roman god Mars come to life and looking for a fight. Well, until he held the kitten in his hand, and then he'd looked...perfect.

Not perfect. No one was perfect.

But the two brothers were tall, dark and handsome. They shared the same brown eyes, but the similarities ended there. One was sexy and dangerous, the black sheep. The other was formal and Old World, the future king.

Jules might be inexperienced when it came to men, but she wasn't stupid. Even if thinking about Alejandro made her pulse quicken, Enrique would make the better husband and father. He was the logical choice, the smart choice.

The only choice.

She was here to be Enrique's bride and his alone. She would be his wife and one day a queen. Whatever she may have felt in Alejandro's arms didn't matter. No one could ever know she found him attractive. As for her fiancé...

So what if he had similar mannerisms and speech as her father? Perhaps Enrique's formality stemmed from nervousness. Crown princes were human, even if few would admit it.

He had selected this room for her. Granted, the view wasn't the one she would have preferred, but he'd had his reasons for choosing it. And he was still better than marrying anyone from Aliestle. Jules smiled genuinely at him. "Thank you for welcoming us into your home."

"It'll be your home soon enough."

She nodded, trying to muster a few ounces of happy feelings and peppiness. She hoped they would come.

"I look forward to seeing you at dinner," he said.

"As do I."

He took her hand and raised it to his mouth. He brushed his lips over her skin.

Jules wanted to feel the same passion and heat she'd felt in Alejandro's arms. She would settle for a spark, tingles, warmth at the point of contact, even a small shiver. But she felt...nothing.

Enrique released her hand. "Until later, my princess."

Later. The word resonated with her.

As he left and closed the door behind him, she remembered what she'd told Izzy, Princess Isabel of Vernonia.

Remember, just because you don't love someone at the beginning doesn't mean you won't love them in the end. Love can grow over time.

Jules needed to listen to her own advice.

My princess. She would be Enrique's princess. She needed to act like it, too.

Just because she didn't feel anything with him now, didn't mean she wouldn't ever. Physical attraction and chemistry weren't the same as love. Passion could be fleeting, but love remained. Prevailed. This first meeting was only the beginning.

Love could grow between her and Enrique.

She had to give the relationship time, keep an open heart and remember how love had blossomed with her parents.

But to be on the safe side until love bloomed with Enrique, Jules realized with an odd pang, keeping her distance from Alejandro would probably be a good idea.

Dinner was exactly what Alejandro thought it would be—a total drag. Each course of the gourmet meal took forever. He enjoyed good food, but by the time the meal finished, he'd be falling out of his chair sound asleep. The conversation about international trade agreements would make a rabbit in heat want to nap.

Across the table, Julianna sat next to her brother, Brandt. She looked stunning in a blue evening gown that matched the color of her eyes. The dress didn't show a lot of skin, but the flowing fabric gave enough of a hint of what was underneath to make a man want to see more.

He tried not to look at her.

Enrique was doing enough staring for both of them.

But Alejandro heard her voice drone on. She tried to sound interested in what others were saying, but her tone lacked warmth. Yes, she was going to be an excellent match for his superficial brother.

Five formally dressed staff members set plates of pan-seared sea scallops in front of each of them at the exact same time. Two wine stewards circled the table filling wineglasses from bottles of Pinot Gris.

What Alejandro wouldn't give for plates of tapas and a pitcher of sangria right now.

Enrique laughed at something Julianna said. So did his father.

"Who knew your bride would be an expert in trade?" Dario said.

"Thank you, sir." Julianna's smile didn't reach her eyes the way it had when she'd petted the kitten. "But trade is a hobby."

A hobby? Maybe a geek lived inside the beauty's body. Or maybe she was trying to impress her future father-in-law. Either way, Alejandro wanted nothing to do with her.

"Now that is a worthy hobby." Enrique pinned Alejandro with a contemptible look. "Unlike *some* of the hobbies others of us have."

He stared over the rim of his wineglass. "Care to wager how my hobby turns out during the Med Cup, bro?"

Julianna's fork clattered against her plate and bounced off the table. Her cheeks turned a bright shade of pink. "Excuse me."

Alejandro studied her. Strange. The stumble in the

foyer aside, Julianna didn't seem like a klutzy princess. It was unusual for someone as elegant as her to drop her fork in the middle of dinner and make a spectacle of herself.

Two servants rushed to her side. One picked up the fork from the ground. The other placed a new fork on the table.

"Thank you." She raised her half-filled water glass. "So you sail, Alejandro?"

"I sail. I also build boats. Racing sailboats." He noticed the glance exchanged between Julianna and Brandt. "Do either of you sail?"

She looked again at her brother.

"We sail," Brandt answered. "On local lakes and rivers. For pleasure. Unlike many of our royal compatriots who enjoy the competitive side of the sport."

Alejandro couldn't understand why Julianna needed her brother to answer such a simple question. She'd had no problem talking about trade.

Enrique swirled the wine in his glass. "Some royals take sailing too seriously. I enjoyed the few regattas I competed in, but I no longer have time to sail with so many other obligations."

"Horse racing may be the sport of kings," Brandt said. "But many royals have sailed for their countries in the Summer Games. I'm sure more would have liked to."

Dario nodded. "I've always preferred the water to horses."

"As have I," Enrique added hastily.

Julianna leaned forward. The neckline of her gown

gaped, giving Alejandro a glimpse of ivory skin and round breasts. He forced his attention onto the sea scallops instead.

"Will one of your boats be entered in the Med Cup?" she asked, as if trying to draw him into conversation.

He appreciated her taking an interest. "My newest design."

"A bit risky, don't you think?" Enrique asked.

Alejandro shrugged. "You never know until you try."

A smug smile curved Enrique's lips. "I may take you up on that wager."

"My sons take the opposite sides on everything," King Dario explained. "And if they can figure a way to bet on the outcome..."

"They sound like my brothers, sir." Julianna's smile lit up her face. The result took Alejandro's breath away. She looked more like the woman he'd held in his arms, not the cool, proper princess. "Brandt isn't as bad as the younger three. At least not any longer."

Brandt raised his glass to her. "Thanks, sis."

"So will you be sailing in the race, Alejandro?" She sounded not only interested but also curious.

"Possibly." The change in her intrigued him. "I'm trying to find the right mix of crew. But the boat can be sailed single-handedly, too."

"Doesn't sound like much of a racing boat," Enrique said.

"The best boats can perform with varying numbers

of crew." Her eyes became more animated as she spoke. "I'm sure it'll be an exciting race."

Alejandro thought he heard a note of wistfulness in her voice. "Racing is always exciting. I'd be happy to take all of you out sailing. You could see the boat for yourself."

Julianna straightened.

Brandt smiled. "Thanks, that sounds like fun."

"Yes, but a sail isn't possible right now." As Enrique spoke, Julianna leaned back in her chair with a thoughtful expression on her face. "I don't need to sail on your boat to know what the outcome of the race will be."

Alejandro didn't know why he tried.

"Enough sailing." Dario gave a dismissive wave of his hand. "We have more important things to discuss, like wedding plans. King Alaric says there is no need for a lengthy engagement."

"Our father is satisfied with the marriage contract," Brandt said. "Whatever wedding date you decide upon is fine with him."

"Outstanding. A short engagement, it'll be." Dario beamed. "How quickly do you two want to get married?"

Enrique and Julianna smiled at each other, but neither said a word.

"If I might make a suggestion, Father," Alejandro offered.

"Go on."

"Set the wedding date a week after the Med Cup, sir."

"That would be a short engagement. Why then?" Dario asked.

"Because two people have never seemed more perfect for each other." Oddly, the words felt like sandpaper against Alejandro's tongue. But the sooner the two were married, the sooner he would be free. "Having the wedding after the Med Cup will allow me to focus all my attention on my responsibilities as best man."

"Excellent suggestion," his father said. "Enrique, Julianna. Do you agree?"

"I do." Enrique stared at Julianna. "I can't wait to marry."

"Neither can I." Julianna sounded like she meant it.

Dario clapped his hands together. The sound echoed through the large dining room. "I'll call King Alaric in the morning."

"I'll start planning our honeymoon," Enrique said.

The thought of Julianna in his brother's bed left a bad taste in Alejandro's mouth. But heirs were necessary if he wanted to be left alone by his father.

Julianna didn't seem to mind. A charming blush crept up her long, graceful neck.

He remembered what Enrique had said about King Alaric's daughter being a virgin. That didn't seem possible unless he had used his wealth to protect her virtue. But was the seemingly in-control princess ready for some passion?

Alejandro couldn't forget the way she'd pressed

into him and how her heart pounded against his chest when he'd held her in his arms or the excited tone of her voice and the gleam in her eyes when she talked about sailing. Only a talented actress could feign that kind of interest.

Maybe there was more to her than Alejandro realized.

Not that it mattered. He picked up his wineglass and sipped. Not much anyway.

CHAPTER THREE

AFTER DINNER, Jules stood out on the terrace alone. Cicadas chirped. A breeze rustled through the palm fronds. The temperature had cooled, but no jacket was required.

She glanced inside through the open terrace doors to see Brandt having a brandy with King Dario. Enrique must still be on his telephone call with the ambassador to the United States.

Jules enjoyed the moment of solitude, a break from the endless conversation at the dinner table. At least the topic had finally turned to something interesting.

With her hands on the railing, Jules gazed up at the night sky. The stars surrounding the almost full moon winked at her. A smile graced her lips.

Perhaps she wasn't cursed.

Enrique hadn't said yes to the sailing invitation, but his words "right now" filled Julianna with hope. He'd raced sailboats. Alejandro built racing sailboats. Her wedding date was a couple of weeks away.

What were the odds of so many things working out so well? Not only was she marrying into a family of sailors, she would soon be Enrique's wife. She could say goodbye to being submissive for the rest of her life.

On La Isla de la Aurora, she would be able to do what she wanted. Personal freedom, yes, but she could also help Brandt to show the world Aliestle was more than an eccentric, backward country. Maybe by doing that, Jules would be able to live up to the spirit of her mother.

Laughter bubbled up inside her.

Oh, she'd visit her homeland, but she would no longer be expected to live by all the restrictive laws and traditions.

The only thing missing was falling in love, but given how well everything else was turning out she believed it would happen. She would fall in love with Enrique and he with her. The same way her parents had fallen in love after their arranged marriage.

It was all going to work out. "I know it will."

"Know what will?" a male voice asked from the shadows.

Jules jumped. "Who's there?"

"I didn't mean to startle you."

She squinted. She couldn't see anyone, but recognized the voice. "Alejandro."

He ascended the staircase leading to the terrace where she stood. "Good evening, Julianna."

Her heart lurched. She fought against the burst of attraction making her mouth go dry. It wasn't easy.

The stubble on his face made him look so much like a sexy pirate. She could easily imagine him standing behind the wheel of a sailing ship trying to capture a vessel full of gold or pretty wenches.

He'd removed his jacket, tie and cummerbund. The neck of his dress shirt was unbuttoned, the tails hung out of the trousers and his sleeves were rolled up. The high rollers decked out in the finest menswear on the Côte d'Azur had nothing on Alejandro. Even with his bare feet.

"How long have you been lurking in the shadows?" she asked.

He moved gracefully like a dancer or a world-class athlete. "Long enough to hear you laughing."

Heat enflamed her cheeks. "If I'd known you were there…"

Alejandro crossed the terrace to stand next to her. "No need to apologize for being happy."

Maybe not for him. But happy wasn't an emotion Jules was used to experiencing let alone expressing. Sharing that moment embarrassed her. Still she owed him for what he'd said at dinner about sailing and the wedding. But one was more important than the other. "Thank you for suggesting a short engagement."

"Afraid you'll change your mind?" he asked.

"Worried Enrique will."

"Not going to happen."

Jules wished she shared Alejandro's confidence. "I've heard that before."

"He'd be a fool, a complete idiot, if he didn't marry you."

His compliment made her feel warm all over. His opinion shouldn't matter, but for some reason it did.

"Well, intelligence has never been a requirement to be a crown prince."

The deep, rich sound of his laughter seeped into her and raised her temperature ten degrees. "You're a contradiction, Julianna."

"How so?"

"Your dress and demeanor present the image of a proper, dutiful princess, who dots her I's and crosses her T's. Yet you show glimpses…"

No one had ever looked beneath the surface or beyond the label of dutiful princess. She wouldn't have expected Alejandro to, either. Full of curiosity, she leaned toward him. "Of what?"

"Of being a not-so-perfect princess."

It was her turn to laugh. That wasn't who she was. Oh, well… Perhaps Enrique would recognize the real her. "You're reading too much into my words and deeds. Women are second-class citizens in Aliestle. We must obey the men in our lives or deal with the consequences. Duty becomes our way of life. But that doesn't mean we don't have the same hopes and dreams, the same sense of humor, as women in more contemporary lands such as this island."

"As I said, a contradiction."

She eyed him warily. "Thank you, I think."

"It's a compliment." He glanced back toward the sitting room. "Your groom has returned."

Jules looked behind her to see Enrique holding a brandy and talking with the others.

"I should leave you." Alejandro took a step toward

the staircase. "I don't want my brother to think I'm trying to steal his princess bride."

Would Alejandro do that? Her pulse skittered thinking he might.

Stop. Now. She couldn't allow herself to be carried away with girlish fantasies. She raised her chin. "Enrique wouldn't think—"

"Yes, he would."

"Have you stolen his girlfriends in the past?"

His eyes raked over her. "No, we have different taste in women."

Alejandro's stark appraisal should have made her feel uncomfortable, but he also made her feel sexy, a way she'd never felt before. She wet her lips. "Would your being the black sheep and all the gossip have something to do with Enrique feeling this way?"

Alejandro grinned wryly. "Possibly."

"So the rumors and stories are true."

"Some are," he admitted. "Others are exaggerations."

He was a gorgeous prince. That often led people to act out of... "I'm sure a few tales are due to jealousy."

He eyed her curiously. "Has this happened to you?"

"Oh, no. I'm about as proper a princess as you'll find."

"Proper with obvious skills of manipulation."

"Proper with practiced social skills and manners that help others get along."

"Yet you downplay your intelligence by saying your

knowledge about international trade is nothing but a hobby."

His perceptiveness made her feel like a mouse caught in a trap. He might be a black sheep and prefer to go barefoot, but he was sharp. She'd have to watch herself. "Education opportunities for females in my country exist, but are limited. Women are allowed to hold only certain jobs. We must work within the system. I've been more fortunate than others and able to use my time traveling abroad to…expand my knowledge base. But the last thing my country wants is their princess spouting off how smart she thinks she is."

Laughter lit Alejandro's eyes and made her temperature rise ten degrees. "You'll be good for Enrique. Keep him on his toes. But he won't mind."

"I hope not. What about you?" Jules liked the easy banter between them. Earlier when she'd arrived, she thought Alejandro didn't like her. "Will you mind not being second in line for the throne after Enrique and I have children?"

He glanced inside once again. "I can honestly say the more children you and my brother are blessed with, the happier I'll be. I've been hoping to be made an uncle for years."

His words sounded genuine. She ignored her disappointment that he wouldn't want her himself. That was stupid. Her father would never approve of a man like Alejandro, and she needed to be a queen to best help Brandt and Aliestle. "That's sweet of you."

"The kitten is sweet. I'm not." He took two steps

down the stairs. "Enrique's on his way out here. That's my cue to fade back into the shadows."

Alejandro's cryptic words intrigued her. "Do you usually hang out in the shadows?"

"Yes, I do."

She watched him disappear into the night.

Behind her, footsteps sounded against the terrace's tile floor. A familiar scent of aftershave enveloped her. She didn't like the fragrance. Still better than the alternative, she reminded herself.

Jules leaned forward over the railing, but couldn't see Alejandro. "I hope your call went well.

"It did." Enrique stood next to her. "But you needn't worry about state business. The wedding should be your focus."

"I've been thinking about our wedding." She wondered if Alejandro was listening from below. Not that she minded if he eavesdropped. A part of her wished he was here with her instead of his brother. "And children, too."

"We are of like minds." Enrique placed his hand over hers. His skin was warm and soft. His nails neatly trimmed. Not the hands of a sailor or gardener. "Heirs would please my father."

"Mine, too." Her duty was to extend the bloodline. But Jules also wanted babies of her own. She remembered helping the nurses with each of her brothers. She wanted to be more involved with raising her children than her stepmother.

Enrique's eyes darkened. "Once we are married we shouldn't waste any time starting a family."

His suggestive tone made her shiver. Not a surprising reaction given she'd never discussed sex with any of her matches before. Offspring had always been assumed. "I would like a big family. At least four children."

He tucked her hair behind her ears. "I hope they all look like you."

His compliment was nice, but the words didn't make her feel warm and fuzzy the way Alejandro's had. "Thank you."

"My brother will be pleased to know you want so many children," Enrique said. "He can't wait to fall lower in the line of succession. I believe if he could give away or relinquish his title he would without a second thought."

"I can't imagine anyone wanting to do that," she admitted. "But Alejandro does have his boats."

She envied his ability to follow his dreams.

"Nothing matters but those damn boats. Sailing has consumed him. He works as a manual laborer, a commoner, refusing to take advantage of the free publicity being a royal engaged in business always brings."

Enrique's critical tone didn't surprise Jules. The two brothers seemed to always be going at each other. But sometimes that might keep them from seeing a situation more clearly. "If Alejandro wins the Med Cup, he'll earn respect. New customers."

"He won't win with a new design," Enrique said. "Competition is fierce. The best crews are going to be on well-known, tested designs. Too bad my brother is too stubborn to use the same boat as last year. But he always wants something newer, better. That's one reason I doubt he'll ever marry. He upgrades the women in his life like they were cars."

The picture Enrique painted of his younger brother was not flattering. Jules wondered if this was one of the stories Alejandro had mentioned. The two brothers needed to get along better. That gave her an idea.

"Sail his other boat for him," she said. "The one he sailed last year."

"I haven't raced since my duties became expanded. State business takes up the majority of my time."

His curt tone rebuked her. "It was only a suggestion."

"Racing in open water isn't without risks."

"I've never sailed in the ocean." Just dreamed about it.

"Your father told me he's forbidden you to sail on the sea. That's why I didn't accept Alejandro's invitation to go sailing."

"You and Brandt can go."

"Not without you," Enrique said, and she appreciated his courtesy. "Your father mentioned your mother's accident. So tragic."

Jules knew information would be exchanged during the marriage negotiations, but she'd never been privy to it. "My mother's death was an accident, a freak occurrence."

"No matter the circumstances." Enrique's voice

softened. "Your father said he was deeply affected by the loss."

"I've been told he changed after she died. He loved my mother very much."

"He loves you, too."

Hearing the words from someone outside her family made Jules feel as if all the sacrifices she'd made to live up to the expectations of her father, family and country had been worth it. Her tongue felt thick, heavy, so she nodded.

"A lesser man might not have recovered from such a tragedy," Enrique continued.

She appreciated the admiration in his words. "My father is a king. He is a strong man. He mourned my mother's death, but he remarried less than a year later. He needed a male heir. I was a young child who needed a mother."

"Understandable."

Jules wondered if that meant Enrique would do the same should she die. Probably. "La Isla de la Aurora seems more progressive than Aliestle."

"It is, though we are a little old-fashioned about a few things," Enrique said. "Do not worry. I intend to make sure you like it here, Julianna.

His words fed her growing hopes. She gathered her courage. "My father said you would decide whether I could sail on the ocean after we are married. You told Alejandro we couldn't sail right now. Does that mean you've given some thought to my sailing after our wedding?"

"Your father also discussed this with me. I've already made my decision."

Her heart raced. She held her breath.

Please, oh, please. Say yes.

Enrique squeezed her hand again. "Sailing on the sea is too dangerous."

Jules felt as if someone had wrapped a line around her heart and pulled hard. She had to make him understand, to see how important this was to her. "I am a careful sailor. I would never take undue risks."

"You are on the ocean. Weather can change. No one, not even the best sailors in the world, can remove all the risk."

She understood that. She wasn't a complete idiot.

Desperate to make this work she sought another test. "Sailing is a pleasurable leisure activity. Something we could do together in our free time."

"I don't have a lot of free time."

"It wouldn't have to be that often. Only once in a while."

"We may have just met, but I must admit I understand your father's concerns." Enrique spoke to her as if she were a child. "You are to be the mother of my children, my wife, my queen. I wouldn't want anything to happen to you as it did your mother."

Disappointment settled in the center of Jules's chest, but she didn't allow her shoulders to slump. Being here was still better than Aliestle. "So I'm only allowed to sail on lakes and rivers?"

"I've seen what sailing has done to my brother.

The sport killed your mother. Once we are married, I do not want you to sail again."

The air rushed from Jules lungs. Tears stung her eyes. She clutched the railing. "But I've always been able to sail. Just not on the ocean."

"That was your father's decision. This is mine."

No! Her chest tightened. This was so much worse than she imagined. It wasn't only the sailing. The tone of Enrique's voice told her she would be exchanging her controlling father for a controlling husband. Her freedom would be curtailed here, too.

"Don't look so disappointed," Enrique chided. "This isn't personal. I'm not trying to be cruel."

"What are you trying to do then?"

"Be honest and help you," he said. "It's time for you to grow up and put childish things aside, Julianna. You may believe sailing is good for you, but it's been brought to my attention that sailing brings out a wilder side in you."

She drew back. "What have I done?"

"Kissed Prince Niko."

"One kiss. We were engaged at the time."

"There have been other reports," Enrique said calmly, as if they were discussing business and not her life. "Such a pursuit is inappropriate for a future queen. You must embrace the bigger duty you'll now have."

Jules forced herself to breathe. Carving a new life for herself and helping Aliestle would be an uphill battle. She would be constrained here on the island, too. "What is to be my role here? My bigger duty?"

"You are to be my wife. You will provide me with heirs."

Both of those things she'd known about. Accepted. But she doubted that was all Enrique would want from her. "And?"

"You will be a conventional princess and queen the people can respect. It's in your best interest to do what I say and not bring any embarrassment to our name."

Her best interest? What about their best interest? Enrique seemed to want to tell her what to do, not have a real relationship with her. How could love grow out of that?

Emotion clogged her throat.

What was she going to do?

Returning to Aliestle in disgrace and marrying a nobleman would be the worst choice for her, Brandt, her country and her future children. Doing something more drastic didn't appeal to her, either.

Other women might run away. But if she turned her back on her responsibilities she would be exiled. Her father would keep her brothers from seeing her. Not only that, her father would also denounce her. Conditions would worsen for the women in her country. She couldn't give up on everything she'd sacrificed her whole life for and her family.

That left one choice—going through with the wedding. Her stomach churned.

Think of the bigger picture, the future, others.

Jules would be able to help Brandt and Aliestle. Her children would have a better life and more choices on the island. Those things would make up for everything she was giving up. In time, Jules would see she made the right decision.

But right now, it still...hurt.

In an apartment on the ground floor, Alejandro tried to relax. But being back at the palace made him antsy. So did something else. Someone else...

Julianna.

Maybe she wasn't as bad as he originally thought. She seemed different tonight, warmer and more genuine. But if that were the case, he couldn't understand her icy facade earlier.

Not that he should be thinking about his brother's fiancée at all.

Alejandro sat on the floor and used a laser pointer to play with the kitten. This was the same room he'd had as a teenager, though the furniture had been replaced, the floors refinished and the walls painted. The decor wasn't the only change. Back when he'd been a teenager, a guard had always been stationed outside the back door that led to the beach path to keep him from running away. Not that a guard had been able to stop him. At least his father hadn't posted anyone there tonight.

The kitten sprinted across the hardwood floor after the red dot, pawing and pouncing until he plopped onto a hand-woven rug and purred. His eyes closed.

As Alejandro moved from the floor to a chair, a flash of blue passed outside the window. The same blue as Julianna's gown.

He stood to get a better look.

Silky fabric and blond hair billowed behind her as she hurried down the path leading to the beach, making her look almost ethereal with the starry night sky as her backdrop.

Not his type, Alejandro reminded himself.

He glanced at the clock. Eleven o'clock. A little late to go beachcombing. Not that what she did was any of his business.

But no one seemed to be with her. Not Enrique. Not her bodyguard.

That didn't sit well with Alejandro.

She shouldn't be alone. It was dark. She could lose her way.

On a lighted path, an inner voice mocked.

Something could happen to her. Alejandro ignored the fact that he could find his brother and send him after Julianna.

Alejandro stepped outside onto the patio. The tile was hard beneath his bare feet. Planters full of fragrant flowers lined the edge. Lanterns hung from tall wrought-iron poles.

Maybe Julianna wanted a closer look at the water, or to dance on the beach under the moonlight...or skinny-dip.

As his blood surged at the thought, he quickened his pace. Now that he would like to see. Ice princess or not.

The lighted path stopped at the beach. Alejandro's bare feet sunk into the fine sand. Thanks to the moonlight, he saw Julianna standing at the water's edge holding her high heels in one hand. The hem of her gown dragged on the sand. Wind ruffled her hair and the fabric of her dress. Waves crashed against the shore, the water drawing closer to her. She didn't move.

Mesmerized by the sea or thinking? About him?

He scoffed at the stupid thought. She would be thinking about Enrique. Her fiancé. Alejandro should leave her alone.

Yet he remained rooted in place, content to watch her.

Being here had nothing to do with the way her dress clung to her curves or the slit that provided him with a glimpse of her long, smooth legs. He was here for her protection. Even though this strip of white sand was private, reachable only from the palace or by water. He didn't see any boats offshore, only silver moonlight reflecting off the crescents of waves.

Still he stood captivated by the woman in front of him. The individual, not incarnations of women she would become. Future sister-in-law, mother of his nieces and nephews, queen.

He longed to go to her, pull her into an embrace, taste her sweet lips and feel her lush curves pressed against him.

What the hell was he thinking?

Disgusted with the fantasy playing in his mind, Alejandro turned to leave. Julianna moved in his peripheral vision. He looked back. She sat on the sand, resting her head in her hands. Her shoulders shook as if she were crying.

A sob smacked into him. His gut clenched.

The instinct to bolt was strong. Tears made him uncomfortable. He'd been in enough short-term relationships to know crying women were to be avoided at all costs. He never knew what to say and feared making a situation worse.

Yet he walked toward her anyway as if pulled by an invisible line. Compelled by something he couldn't explain. "Julianna."

She didn't look up. "Go away, please."

Her voice sounded raw, yet she was polite, always the proper princess. He saw her behavior wasn't an act like his brother's. His respect inched up for her. "I'm not going away."

"I'll pretend you aren't here then."

"It won't be the first time that's happened." He plopped onto the sand next to her. "I've been becalmed many times. Having the boat bob like a cork while waiting for wind to return used to drive me crazy, but I've learned to enjoy the downtime."

She remained silent.

As waves broke against the shore, Alejandro studied the stars in the sky. He drew pictures in the sand. A boat. A crab. A heart. He wiped them away with the side of his hand.

Julianna raised her head. "You're still here."

"Yes." Tears streaked her cheeks. The sadness in her swollen eyes reignited his desire to take her in his arms and kiss her until she smiled. "I may have some of the same stubborn streak shared by other members of my family."

She sniffled.

He wished he had a tissue for her. One of those handkerchiefs his brother and father carried in their pockets would come in handy. "When you're ready to talk..."

A new round of tears streamed down her face. She looked devastated, as if someone she loved had died.

Her vulnerability clawed at his heart, made him feel useless, worthless. He couldn't sit here and do nothing.

Alejandro turned toward Julianna and lifted her onto his lap.

She gasped. Stiffened.

A mistake, probably, but he'd deal with that later. He needed to help Julianna.

The moment he wrapped his arms around her something seemed to release inside her. She sagged against him, rested her head on his shoulder and cried. He rubbed her back with his hand, the same way his mother used to do whenever he'd been hurt by something Enrique did or his father had said.

Julianna's tears didn't stop, but that didn't bother Alejandro. She felt so perfect nestled against him. Her sweet scent enveloped him. He would have preferred to be in this position under different circumstances, but he knew that wasn't possible. She had a fiancé—what she needed tonight was a friend.

He could be a friend. That was all he could ever be to her.

Her tears slowed. Her breathing became less ragged.

"Thank you," Julianna muttered. "I'm sorry for inconveniencing you. This is so unlike me."

Alejandro brushed the strands of hair sticking to her tearstained cheeks. "You're in my arms and on my lap. Formalities and apologies aren't necessary."

She stared up at him. Even with puffy, red eyes she was still beautiful.

But she was almost family. She would be his sister-in-law.

Julianna scooted off his lap. "I'm better now."

He missed the warmth of her body, the feel of her curves against him. "Tell me what's wrong."

She looked at the water. "It's nothing."

"Let me be the judge of that."

A beat passed. And another. "Did you hang around after Enrique joined me on the terrace?"

"No." Maybe Alejandro should have.

She took a slow breath. "I thought coming here and marrying Enrique would be so much better than staying in Aliestle. I believed things would be... different."

"I don't understand."

"It's difficult to explain. Do you recall at dinner when you asked if we sailed, and Brandt answered?"

Alejandro nodded. He'd thought that odd.

"Brandt spoke because he knows how much sailing means to me, and I would've gotten carried away. I love it. I'd rather sail than do anything. Being on a boat is the only time I can be myself. Not a proper princess or a dutiful daughter and sister." She gazed at the water. "It's heaven on earth for me."

The passion in her words heated the blood in his veins. The longing for independence, for a freedom from all the expectations of being a royal matched the desire in his heart. This perfect princess was as much a black sheep as him. She just kept the true color of her wool hidden. "I know exactly how you feel."

She studied him. "I thought you might. My father has never allowed me to sail on the ocean due to my mother dying during a race. That's why Enrique turned down your invitation to go sailing. My father said once I married, Enrique could decide whether I could sail or not."

"You'll be living on an island," Alejandro said. "Why wouldn't you sail?"

"That's what I thought. After you left the terrace, I asked Enrique about being able to sail." Her lower lip quivered. "He has forbidden me to sail. Not only on the ocean, but ever again. He says sailing brings out a wildness in me that's not appropriate for a future queen. I'm to be a conventional wife and princess."

Tears gleamed in her eyes.

Damn Enrique. His brother was a complete moron. A total ass. As usual. "He has spoken without thinking."

"He was quite serious about his expectations of me."

"My brother might be a cad, but he isn't a monster. He'll come around."

Tears slipped from the corners of her eyes. "I don't think he will."

Alejandro's chest tightened. "I'll talk to Enrique. Make him see how much sailing means to you."

"No," she said. "He might change his mind about marrying me."

Not likely given her dowry. But Julianna was so much more than the money she brought to the marriage. She might act like a cold, dutiful princess, but underneath the perfect facade was a passionate woman looking to break free of the obligations that came with her tiara and scepter. La Isla de la Aurora deserved a queen like Julianna. Too bad Enrique didn't deserve a woman like her.

"Ask to be released from the marriage contract." Alejandro couldn't believe those words had come from his lips.

"I can't."

"You won't."

"If I don't marry Enrique, I'll be sent home to marry one of the sons of our Council of Elders." The way her voice cracked hurt Alejandro's heart. "In Aliestle, it's against the law to disobey your husband. I'd rather raise my children in a country that is more progressive. At least in principle. This is my fate. I must learn to accept it."

Alejandro hated seeing her so distressed. She deserved to be happy, to have the freedom to do what she wanted to do.

"Not so fast," he said. "In spite of a few traditional mindsets here, La Isla de la Aurora is a progressive country. That includes our laws. Enrique can't throw you in prison or lock you away in a tower if you disobey him and go sailing."

"This isn't only about my sailing."

"I'm not only talking about sailing. My mother left the island fifteen years ago." Alejandro had learned an important lesson the day his mother left. Never rely on anyone but yourself. "Separation is an option here, even for royals."

"That's very modern compared to where I come from." She wiped her eyes. "You see, I'd hoped to use my position as future queen to effect change back home without embarrassing my country and family."

Alejandro remembered what she'd told him. "Working within the system."

She nodded. "Royals can't be selfish and ignore the people who look up to them."

"That's noble of you," Alejandro said. Too bad most royals didn't feel that way. "But you shouldn't be too upset. My brother's pulling one of his power plays with you. He's done it to me many times and will change his mind. Your life will be better here than in Aliestle. You'll have royal obligations, but you'll also be able to do what you want to do, including help your country and sail."

Her shoulders remained slumped. "Enrique could annul the marriage if I defy him. I'd have to return to Aliestle."

"I don't see a ring on your finger."

"Not yet anyway." She glanced at her left hand. Straightened. "No ring."

"What?" Alejandro asked.

Her gaze met his. "Maybe Enrique will change his mind about things or maybe he won't. I can't change anything that will happen once I marry. But if I go sailing now, I wouldn't be disobeying my husband since Enrique is only my fiancé."

Her tone sounded different. Not as distraught. "You lost me."

Julianna's gaze met Alejandro's with an unspoken plea.

Understanding dawned. He leaned away from her. "No. No way. I can't get involved in this."

"You're already involved." She scooted closer. "All I need is a boat for one sail."

The flowery scent of her shampoo filled his nostrils and made him waver. He leaned backed to put some distance between them. "If you're caught disobeying your father…"

"I'll make sure I'm not," she said. "You believe Enrique will change his mind, but you didn't see the look in his eyes. It's worth the risk for one last hurrah before I get married."

"Maybe to you, but not to me." Alejandro would be in deep trouble. That had never bothered him in the past. But the stakes were higher this time.

"What do you have to lose?" she asked.

His chance at freedom. He hated the way Enrique was treating Julianna, but Alejandro didn't want to cause an even bigger problem between the couple. He needed the two to marry and have children.

A deep shame rose up inside him. He was thinking of himself while Julianna was trying to do her duty even if it made her unhappy.

"I'm sorry," he said. "But I won't be the reason you get in trouble."

Disappointment shone in her lovely eyes.

"Fine." She flipped her hair behind her shoulder with a sexy move. "I'll find a boat myself."

She would, too. He pictured her heading to the marina and going out with anyone who'd take her. That could end in disaster. If he helped her…

Alejandro couldn't believe he was contemplating taking her out, but he didn't want to think only of himself. "Sailing is that important to you?"

"Yes."

The hope and anticipation in the one word made it difficult for him to breath.

"Please, Alejandro." Julianna stared up at him with her wide, blue eyes. "Will you please help me?"

A long list of reasons why he shouldn't scrolled through his mind. But logic didn't seem to apply in this situation. Or with Julianna.

He thought about it a minute. Taking her sailing wasn't that big a deal. "I suppose it would be against my character and ruin my bad reputation if I turned down an opportunity to do something Enrique was against."

She leaned toward him giving him another whiff of her enticing scent. "So is that a yes?"

CHAPTER FOUR

YES. I'll take you sailing tomorrow night.

Jules fell asleep thinking about Alejandro's words. She woke up with them on her mind, too.

Sunlight streamed through the windows. Particles in the air gave the rays definition, as if a fairy had waved her magic wand to make the sunshine touchable. She reached out, but felt only air.

With a laugh, she rolled over in the queen-size bed eager to start her day. She couldn't wait to go sailing tonight. Of course if she was discovered...

Don't think about that.

She needed to do this. Everything else in her life, from her education to her marriage, had been determined for her. Not out of love, but because of what tradition dictated and what others believed to be best for Aliestle.

Going sailing tonight was the one decision she could make for herself. She was desperate enough for this one act of disobedience. A secretive rebellion of sorts, the kind she never did as a teenager.

Jules tossed back the luxurious Egyptian cotton sheet and climbed out of bed. Her bare feet sunk into a hand-woven Persian rug. Only the finest furnishings for the grand palace.

She entered the large bathroom. Yvette had set out her toiletries on the marble countertop. The gold plated fixtures reminded Jules of every other castle she'd stayed in. Gold might be considered opulent, but didn't any of the royal interior designers want to be creative and try a different finish? Then again, royalty could never be too creative or different. The status quo was completely acceptable.

Jules stared at her refection in the mirror. Today she would maintain that status quo. People would look at her and see a dutiful princess. Even if she would be counting down the hours until her first and last taste of…

Freedom.

Her chest tightened. She had no idea what true freedom would feel like.

So far, Jules's choices in life had been relegated to what she wanted to eat, if it wasn't a state dinner, what books she wanted to read, if she'd completed all her assigned readings, and what she purchased while shopping. Perhaps that was why she'd become a consummate shopper.

Choosing what she wanted to do without having to consider the expectations of an overprotective father and a conservative country would have to feel pretty good. She couldn't wait to experience it tonight.

Jules had thought about what Alejandro said about the island not being Aliestle, about the legal rights she would have here and about his mother leaving his father. Those things had led her to devise a new plan.

She would sail tonight, then return to being a dutiful princess in the morning and marry Enrique after the Med Cup. Once they had children, she would work to improve her position, get Enrique to be more cooperative and try to change things.

Thirty minutes later, Yvette clasped a diamond and pearl necklace around Jules's neck. "Excellent choice, Yvette. You have quite an eye when it comes to accessories."

"Thank you, ma'am." The young maid stared at their reflection in the mirror. "You look like a modern day Princess Grace."

Jules felt a little like Princess Grace, who had been forced to stop acting because someone said the people of Monaco wouldn't be happy if she returned to making movies. Life for many royals didn't always have a happy ending.

"Thank you, Yvette." The retro-style pink-and-white suit had been purchased on a recent trip to Paris. Jules tucked a strand of hair into her French twist. "I'm sure the hairstyle helps."

"Prince Enrique will be impressed."

"Let's hope so." Jules tried to sound cheerful, but the words felt flat. She doubted Enrique would be impressed by anything she did. He was nothing like… Alejandro.

She couldn't imagine Enrique cradling her in his arms, offering sympathy while she cried. He would have cursed her tears, not wiped them away as Alejandro had.

A black sheep? Perhaps, but he was taking her sailing. She guessed he was more of a good guy than he claimed to be.

She smiled. "Perhaps I'll make an impression on the entire royal family."

"Not Prince Alejandro." Yvette sounded aghast. "I've been told to stay away from him."

The words offended Jules. She would rather spend time with Alejandro than Enrique. "Who said that?"

"One of the housekeepers. She's young. Pretty," Yvette explained. "She said Prince Alejandro has a horrible reputation. Worse, his taste in women is far from discriminating. Royalty, commoner, palace staff, it doesn't matter."

Alejandro had warned her about the gossip. But the words stung for some reason. "That could be a rumor. The press loves to write about royalty whethe[r] it's true or not. People will believe almost anythir[g] once it's in print or on the Internet."

"The housekeeper sounded sincere, ma'am," Yv[ette] said. "She's especially concerned about you."

"About me?" Jules remembered the warm[th] Alejandro's body and the sense of belonging [she] felt in his arms. He could have taken advant[age of] the situation and her emotional state last ni[ght but] he hadn't. He'd acted like a friend, not a m[an who] wanted some action. She'd actually been [a little] disappointed he hadn't found her desirabl[e]

Silly. Pathetic, really. She straightened. "I appreciate the warning, but I'm going to be Alejandro's sister-in-law. He doesn't see me in the same way as he sees other woman."

Doubt filled Yvette's eyes. "I hope you're correct, ma'am."

Jules didn't. She wouldn't mind being wrong about this. Alejandro was…attractive, but the way he'd made her feel on the beach—understood, accepted, safe, ways she'd never felt before—intrigued her the most. After tonight, following the housekeeper's advice and staying away from him would be the best course of action. No matter how much a tiny part of Jules wished he were the one she was marrying.

Better squelch that thought. Alejandro was going to be her brother-in-law. Nothing else.

"Don't worry." She raised her chin. "I'm not about to risk my match with Enrique for a fling with a self-avowed black sheep."

Even one who was gorgeous and sailed and sent tingles shooting through her. More reasons to keep her distance.

After tonight.

Tonight would be her first chance to experience freedom. The initial step in figuring out how to be an influential princess and her own person.

"That is smart." The tight lines around Yvette's mouth relaxed a little. "Being matched to a man outside Aliestle would be a dream come true for most of our countrywomen, ma'am."

Be careful what you wish, or in this case, ask for.

Jules recognized the maid's wistful tone. She'd sounded the same way on more than one occasion. The weight on her shoulders felt heavier. She wanted life to be different for her countrywomen. "Has a match been secured for you?"

"Yes, ma'am. A very good match." Yvette gave a half smile. "One that will be advantageous to my family."

"That's excellent."

"Yes, ma'am. We marry in two years, after I complete my obligations on the palace staff." The look in Yvette's eyes didn't seem to agree with her words. "I am…most fortunate."

Most likely as fortunate as Jules. Her heart ached. She wanted men to treat the women of Aliestle with respect, consideration and love. Not like commodities.

When Brandt became king…

Yvette adjusted her starched, white apron. "I transferred the contents of your handbag into the purse, ma'am."

"Thank you, I'll…"

A high-pitched noise sounded outside the bedroom door. Not quite a squeal, but not a squeak, either.

Yvette's forehead creased. "It sounds like a baby, ma'am."

Jules hurried to the door and opened it. The noise sounded again. She glanced around the empty hallway. A black ball of fur scratched at the door across the hall.

"You're correct, Yvette. It is a baby. A baby cat."

Jules picked up the kitten who pawed at her. A long, white hair above his right eye bounced like an antenna in the wind. "I can't imagine someone let you out into this big hallway on purpose. Did you escape again?"

The kitten stared up at her with clear, green eyes.

Her heart bumped. She'd always wanted a pet. This one was adorable.

"I can see where he belongs, ma'am," Yvette offered.

"I'll return him." The kitten wiggled in Jules's hands. She cuddled him closer in hopes of settling him down. He rested his head against her arm and purred. "I know where he belongs."

With Alejandro.

Anticipation spurted through her. She wanted to see him. Because of the sailing, she rationalized. That was the only reason. Anything else would be too... dangerous.

"Cat?" Alejandro checked the closet, the bathroom, under the bed and beneath the other furniture. No sight of the furball anywhere.

The kitten didn't come running as he usually did.

Maybe he was locked in the bathroom? Alejandro checked. No kitty.

The last time he'd seen the kitten was before his shower. He glanced around the apartment again. A vase with colorful fresh- cut flowers caught his eye. Those were new.

Only Ortiz knew about the kitten. If whoever delivered the flowers had left the door to the apartment open, the kitten could have gotten out.

Alejandro ran to the door and jerked it open.

Julianna stood in the doorway.

He froze, stunned to see her.

A smile graced her glossed lips. Clear, bright eyes stared back at him. Her pastel-pink suit made her look like the definition of the word princess in the dictionary.

She was the image of everything he didn't like in a woman—royal, wealthy, concerned with appearances. He shouldn't feel any attraction toward Julianna whatsoever. But he couldn't stop staring at her beautiful face.

Awareness buzzed through him. Strange. Alejandro didn't usually go for the prim and proper type. But this wasn't the time to examine his attraction to her. He needed to find a kitten. "I—"

"I was about to knock," she said at the same time. "Look who I found."

Alejandro followed her line of sight. The kitten was sound asleep in her arms.

Relief washed over him. "I was on my way out to look for him. Where did you find him?"

"In the hallway trying to squeeze under the door across from mine. A futile effort given his size, but he made a valiant attempt." She smiled at the kitten. "I figured he must have escaped and you'd want him back."

"Yes." Alejandro tried focusing on the cat, but

his gaze kept returning to her. He wanted to chalk his reaction to her up to gratitude but knew better. "Thanks."

"You're welcome."

Alejandro waited for Julianna to hand over the cat. She didn't. He needed to go to the boatyard, but he wasn't in that much of a hurry. He motioned into the apartment. "Please come in."

Julianna looked to her left and then to the right. "Thanks, but I'd better not."

He gave her a puzzled look. "You have plans."

"No," she admitted. "I don't want to upset Enrique."

Alejandro ignored the twinge of disappointment. He understood her concern. "You're right. We don't want to add fuel to the fire."

"Especially with tonight," she whispered. Excitement danced in her eyes.

He was looking forward to the sail. He wanted Julianna to like it here. For his sake as much as hers. She'd realize she wouldn't be a prisoner on the island. Enrique didn't know how to treat women properly; a combination of selfishness and lack of experience. His brother would settle down eventually.

"Rest up today or you'll be exhausted," Alejandro said.

"Like the kitten. He fell asleep on the walk over here. He must have tired himself out during his adventure."

Alejandro wouldn't mind tiring himself out with Julianna. He imagined her beautiful long hair loose and spread across his pillow, her silky skin against his, the taste of those lips…

His blood heated and roared through his veins.

He pushed the fantasy out of his mind. Thinking of Julianna in a sexual way was wrong and dangerous. They both had too much to lose.

"I've been wondering what the kitten's name is," she said.

Good, he could think about something other than her in his bed. "Cat."

"Cat is the kitten's name?"

"Yes."

Julianna drew her delicately arched eyebrows together. Her pretty pink mouth opened then closed, as if she thought better of what she wanted to say.

"What?" he asked.

"It's nothing."

Alejandro recognized the look in her eyes. "Tell me."

Julianna hesitated. "You're doing me a favor taking me sailing. I shouldn't criticize."

He'd been criticized his entire life by his father and by his brother. He never could live up to what the people wanted him to be, either. The bane of being the spare. Nothing he did was ever good enough. Alejandro had grown immune to the put-downs. "I want to know."

"You might get mad."

He didn't want her to be afraid of him. "Enrique might get a little heated at times. You don't have to worry about that with me."

MELISSA McCLONE
85

She squared her shoulders, as if preparing for battle. A one-hundred-eighty-degree difference from her sobbing on the beach last night. "Cat isn't a proper name for a pet."

That was what this was all about. Alejandro almost laughed. He thought it was something serious. "Cat doesn't seem to mind the name."

"That's because he loves you."

The warmth in her voice wrapped around Alejandro like a soft, fluffy towel. He couldn't remember the last time anyone had made him feel so good. But he knew better. The feeling was as fleeting as the love she spoke about. "Love has nothing to do with it. He's a cat. He comes because he's hungry."

"He'd come no matter what you call him," she continued.

"Cat isn't a child."

"No, he's your pet."

Children and a family weren't something he'd considered before. Saying he had a pet was pushing the level of commitment he was comfortable with. Love and commitment didn't last so why bother? His mother had claimed to love him. But she'd abandoned him to a father who disapproved of him and a brother who antagonized him. Alejandro rocked back on his heels. "Cat's a stray."

"Living in a palace."

Her voice teased. Okay, she had a point. "If I give the cat a proper name, I'll have to keep him."

She pursed her lips. "Do you plan on releasing him when he gets bigger?"

Alejandro fought the urge to squirm under her scrutiny. He hadn't done anything wrong or irresponsible. At least not yet. "I haven't thought that far ahead. But cats take off when they get tired of you."

She peered around him and motioned to the sock tied in a knot, piece of rope and empty boxes strewn across the floor. "You're going to need to buy a suitcase when he goes so he can take his toys with him."

"I just had that stuff lying around." Alejandro shoved his hands in his pockets. "I'll probably keep him. At the boatyard when he gets older," he clarified.

"Then you might as well come up with a more original name for him."

"He's a cat. The name fits."

"True, but look at his green eyes. His handsome face. The white boots on his paws." She held the kitten up as if he were a rare treasure. "He is so much more than a generic cat."

Alejandro laughed, enchanted by her tenacity. "If you ever get tired of being a princess, you should become a trial lawyer."

She scrunched her nose. "I've never considered such a career, but I would be happy to provide more evidence for changing the kitten's name."

"For someone who wants *me* to take them sailing," he lowered his voice, "you're not very agreeable."

Her eyes widened. Her complexion paled. "Oh, I'm—"

"Kidding." Alejandro didn't think she would take

him seriously. But he could make it up to her. He thought about her description of the kitten. One word popped out at him. "Boots."

A line creased above her nose. "Excuse me?"

"Cat's name is now Boots. Satisfied?"

"Very." She smiled, visibly relieved. "Thank you."

Pleasing her felt better than it should. Just trying to make her happy so she'd want to marry Enrique.

Yeah, right. Alejandro leaned against the doorjamb. "It's the least I could do after the way you argued for his rights. Perhaps you should do the same for your own. And your countrywomen."

Her smile disappeared. So did the light from her eyes. He didn't like the change in her.

"I would if I could, but that's not the kind of princess Aliestle or your brother wants." She touched one of the kitten's small paws. Her expression softened. "The least I could do was support a fellow underdog."

"I don't think Boots would like to be associated with anything having to do with a dog."

The corners of her mouth slanted upward. "You're probably right about that."

Alejandro reached out to pet the kitten. His fingers brushed against the bare skin on Julianna's arm. Tingles shot outward from the point of contact. He jerked his hand away.

She didn't seem to notice.

Good. He didn't want her to know she had an effect on him. "You like cats."

"I do, but I've never had one." She rubbed the top of the kitten's head. "My father didn't want any animals in the palace. He claimed they were too dirty and too much trouble."

Alejandro hadn't expected to have anything else in common with her except sailing. "We had a dog growing up, but after she died my father didn't want another one. He said dogs were too much trouble."

Julianna eyed him with curiosity. "Yet you have Boots."

But Alejandro didn't live in the palace. He doubted his family would want Julianna to know he was here for appearance sake and would be departing after the wedding. "Black sheep, remember?"

"I haven't forgotten. I hope your reputation means you're an expert at subterfuge and not getting caught."

He winked. "You're in experienced hands, Princess."

"Excellent." The sparkle returned to her eyes. She glanced behind her as if to make sure they were still alone. "Have all the arrangements been made?"

The princess's hushed voice made it sound as if they were going to undertake an important, secretive mission. Alejandro realized in her mind they were. The least he could do was play along.

"Almost," he whispered back. "Check your closet this afternoon. Everything you need for tonight will be in there."

Her mouth formed a perfect O. "My closet? You're going to go into my room. Isn't that risky?"

"No one will see me."

"You can't be certain. My maid might be—"

"There are secret tunnels and passageways through-out the palace." He didn't want her to worry. "You access them through hidden latches in the closets."

"Oh."

The one word spoke volumes of her doubt.

"Do you trust me?" he asked.

She handed the kitten to him. "I don't have a choice if I want to go sailing."

"No, you don't."

Alejandro felt like a jerk. He was the last person she should be putting her faith in. He had the most to gain by her marrying Enrique. She had the most to lose by saying "I do." Okay, his brother wasn't that bad. But she was still sacrificing for the marriage.

"Not many people would understand how impor-tant tonight is to me," she said. "I trust you won't let me down."

He appreciated her earnest expression and words. He was used to those in the palace being unable to see past his rebellions as a teen and his wanting to change the monarchy from the archaic monolith it had become.

But Julianna was far too trusting. She must have lived a sheltered life in Aliestle. Things would be better for her on the island. "You're the perfect fairy-tale princess."

Defiance flashed in her eyes, but disappeared quickly. "A princess, yes. Perfect, not so much. Though I try my best."

"Trying is an admirable trait, but not if it makes you unhappy."

"Doing what is expected of me is all I know."

Julianna was nothing like he imagined she would be. She wasn't jaded in spite of being a royal prisoner her entire life. She was the closest thing to perfection he'd ever met. Alejandro would make sure Enrique treated her fairly. "You do a good job."

She rewarded him with a closemouthed smile. He would have preferred to see one with her straight, white teeth visible. "I plan to continue to do so."

Except tonight.

Crossing the line had become second nature to him growing up. Alejandro didn't do it as often now. Still he didn't care what anyone thought about him. The lovely princess did care. The way she dressed, spoke and acted made it clear. She might feel the need to rebel in this one-time act of defiance. A brief escape from an impending arranged marriage and a curtailed freedom. But he didn't want Julianna to have any regrets over what they were going to do.

"Are you certain you want to go against your father and sail tonight?" Alejandro whispered.

"Most definitely.

"You may regret—"

"I'll regret not doing so more," she interrupted. "This is the right thing to do. Even if I'm caught."

Julianna was saying the right words. Alejandro hoped she meant them. Because if she got caught, the price she would pay might be higher than either of them imagined.

* * *

That evening, the hands on the clock in the dining room moved slower than the Council of Elders. King Dario sat at the head of the table. His two sons sat on his left with Jules and Brandt on the king's right.

She tapped her foot, impatient the meal was taking so long. Servers scurried about with wine bottles and platters. She wanted dinner to end so she could excuse herself and prepare for the sail with Alejandro.

He sat across the table from her. No tuxedo, but a designer suit and dress shirt sans tie. He looked more like a CEO than a boatbuilder. Well, except for his hair. The dark ends brushed his shoulders. She preferred his casual, carefree style to Enrique's short, conservative cut.

She kept hoping Alejandro would say something to turn the dinner conversation away from the upcoming royal wedding and onto something more interesting.

He didn't. He barely spoke or glanced her way.

No doubt trying to keep anyone from guessing about the rendezvous later. Jules suppressed the urge to smile about her impending adventure.

King Dario yawned. "I'm going to skip having a brandy."

Alejandro straightened. "Are you feeling okay, Father?"

The king waved off his son's genuine concern. "I'm fine. Just tired."

"Dealing with the demands of the island takes a lot out of a person." Enrique narrowed his gaze as he spoke to Alejandro. "Something you would know little about, brother."

Jules waited for Alejandro to fire back a smart-assed comment. He took a sip of wine instead. When he finished, he wiped his mouth with a napkin. His dark eyes revealed nothing of his thoughts. "Sleep well, Father."

With that, King Dario departed.

Silence filled the dining room. The servers seemed to have vanished along with the king. Jules counted to one hundred by tens in Japanese. When could she say good-night without drawing suspicions to herself?

"I have work to attend to." Enrique scooted his chair away from the table. "If you do not mind," he said to her as if an afterthought.

Perfect! Her entire body felt as if it were smiling. "I don't mind."

"I was planning to hit the clubs," Brandt said with eager anticipation in his voice.

Yes! She couldn't have arranged this any better if she'd planned it. "Take Klaus with you."

Brandt rolled his eyes.

"Listen to your sister," Alejandro suggested. "You'll be thankful you have a bodyguard should things get out of hand."

"My brother knows the island's club scene intimately." Derision dripped from each of Enrique's word. "He's often at the center of the melees."

Jules didn't like his tone. She often gave her four brothers a hard time and teased them, like any big sister, but she never spoke with such disrespect.

"Please, Brandt," she said. "Father would never forgive me if something happened to you."

"And vice versa." Brandt directed a warm smile full of love her way. "I'll have Klaus accompany me."

Relieved, she smiled at him. "Thank you."

Enrique remained seated in his chair, but he looked ready to bolt out any minute. She wished he'd go.

"What will you do tonight, Julianna?" he asked.

"Oh, I don't know." She forced herself not to look at Alejandro. "Read. Watch TV. I'll find something to do."

She wiggled her toes in anticipation of what she would actually be doing.

Enrique rose from the table. "Then I'll bid you good-night and see you tomorrow."

Jules watched him exit the dining room. The atmosphere seemed less stuffy with Enrique gone. Her uncharitable thought brought a stab of guilt. He was her future husband. She'd best accept him as he was.

Alejandro rose. "I'm going to say good-night, also."

"Will I see you later?" Brandt asked.

"Not tonight," Alejandro said. "I have a prior engagement."

Yes, he did. She bit back a smile. In two hours and twenty-two minutes she would meet him at a private dock. The map, a headlamp and everything else she needed were sitting inside a duffel bag she'd found in her closet this afternoon.

"Blonde or brunette?" Brandt asked.

Alejandro laughed at the innuendo. "I wish I could say differently, but unfortunately it's not that kind of…engagement."

Jules tried to figure out what Alejandro meant. That he wished he were seeing a different woman or he wished he were meeting her under different circumstances? Not that he would or she could. But still…

"You can meet me at a club later," Brandt said.

Alejandro glanced her way. "Maybe I will."

"No." The two men looked at her with surprised expressions. Jules's heart dropped to her feet. She hadn't meant to say the word out loud. "I mean, do you know how long you'll be, Alejandro? Brandt might not want to stick around one club waiting for you to show up."

Brandt shook his head. "Stop being such a big sister, Jules. He can text me when he arrives."

"Oh, right," she said. "You know how often I go clubbing."

"You've never been to a club," Brandt said.

She'd never been allowed to go. She always wondered if her bodyguards were more concerned protecting her or ensuring she remained a virgin so her father could use that in marriage negotiations. "Exactly."

"Your sister's correct, though," Alejandro said. "I have no idea how long I'll be. I may not make it."

Brandt shrugged. "More lovely ladies for me."

"Save some for us tomorrow night."

Her brother grinned. "You're on."

Jules didn't want to think about tomorrow and

the life waiting for her as Enrique's bride and future queen. She wanted tonight to last forever. She wanted it to start now.

She rose from the table. "Good night, gentlemen. I hope you enjoy the rest of your evening."

"I hope you're not too bored here alone," Brandt said.

"Don't worry. I won't be bored at all." Her gaze met Alejandro's for a moment. "Tonight is exactly what I need."

CHAPTER FIVE

TWO HOURS LATER, Jules stood in the walk-in closet in her room. The headlamp she wore illuminated the dark space. She wore sailing clothes two sizes too big, a short, dark wig and a cap. She clutched a map in her left hand. With a steadying breath, she searched for the hidden latch with a trembling right hand.

She'd never disobeyed her father or anyone else for that matter. She'd never come close to doing anything illicit unless you counted eating an entire bag of chocolate in one sitting. But this...

Her heart pounded against her chest.

You're in experienced hands, Princess.

Alejandro's words gave her a needed boost of courage.

Jules's fingers brushed across something. She sucked in a breath. The latch. She pressed the small, narrow lever. Something squealed. She stepped backward. A secret door opened to reveal a staircase.

Her insides quivered with a mix of nerves and excitement and a little fear.

She stood at the threshold and glanced down the

pitch-black stairwell. The headlamp illuminated the narrow steps.

Jules ventured forward onto the first step with a slight hesitation. Nerves bubbled in her tummy. She found a latch on the inside of the passageway and closed the secret door.

The steep staircase led to a tunnel that looked as if it had been there for decades, possibly a century or more. She wondered what the tunnel had been used for in the past. Had other princesses used it to escape?

Her feet carried her across a packed dirt floor. Weathered, thick wood beams reinforced the walls and ceiling. The map said the tunnel was two kilometers long. The distance felt longer with the inky shadows stretching out in front of her.

Something gray darted across the floor at the edge of the headlamp beam.

Her breath caught in her throat. She shivered with a sense of foreboding. Nothing like being in an underground tunnel with rodents for companionship.

Not rodents, she corrected. Mice.

"No rats in the palace," she muttered. "No rats in the palace."

With the words as her mantra, Jules continued forward. Adrenaline quickened her pace. More creatures scurried across the floor or ran along the walls. Her nerves increased. She wanted out of here. Now.

She came to a wrought-iron gate secured with a combination lock. She pulled the lock toward her and dialed in the digits written on the map: 132823. The lock clicked open.

The sound of freedom.

Jules opened the gate and stepped through with all the excitement of Christmas morning back when she was a child. She exited the tunnel and found herself in a grotto. No one would ever guess inside one of the rocks was a secret tunnel. She memorized the spot where she'd come out.

Following a paved path, her apprehension rose. She had no idea where she was. Insects chirped and buzzed. But she saw no people, no other lights.

Keep going.

Alejandro had planned the outing so she wouldn't get caught. A good thing, Jules knew. She trusted him for the reason she'd told him. She had no other choice if she wanted to sail. She couldn't have pulled this off on her own in spite of her bravado on the beach last night.

She continued walking, unable to shake her uneasiness at being out here secluded yet exposed. Not that she was about to turn around. This opportunity was too important.

Being out here alone, without servants, bodyguards, chaperones or family, was something she rarely got to do. She might be fighting nerves, but the experience gave her a little thrill.

The canopy and walls of rocks gave way to a large field of grass with gardens on either side. The moonlight eased some of her anxiety.

The path led her up a rise. She heard the sound

of waves crashing against the shore. At the top, she stopped, mesmerized by the sight of the sea. The beach had to be below her somewhere, but she focused on the water. Light from the full moon shimmered like silver on the crests of the waves.

Jules's breath caught in her throat.

So beautiful.

As she descended the path toward the water, she noticed a light shining. A lone lamppost stood on a short dock with a sailboat moored at the end.

Her pulse rate quadrupled, as did her excitement. She'd found the place without getting lost or caught.

Jules hurried down the path, eager to hop onboard and set sail.

A figure stood in the cockpit of the boat. A man. Alejandro. Her heart gave a little lurch of pleasure.

He waved.

Jules waved back.

Alejandro reached below deck. The running lights illuminated—red on port, green on starboard and white on the stern.

Exhilaration shimmied through her. She could forget about duty and obligation tonight. She could be herself and sail on the ocean like a bird set free from its cage.

With Alejandro.

He motioned for her to join him in the boat.

Shoulders back. Chin up. Smile.

This time it came naturally. No effort required.

Jules turned off her headlamp. She no longer needed the light with the lamppost on the dock.

Tingles filled her stomach. She couldn't imagine sharing tonight with anyone else.

As Julianna walked along the private dock with a clear spring to her step, the tension in Alejandro's shoulders eased. He'd planned her escape from the palace with the precision of a military operation. His efforts had seemed to work. With one foot in the cockpit and the other on the rail, he waited for her to come to him.

She stopped two feet away from the boat. "Your map was spot-on, Alejandro."

He liked the way his name rolled off her tongue. She might sound like the same elegant princess he'd met yesterday, but she looked nothing like the woman who had stared down her nose at him, cried in his arms on the beach and prompted him to rename his cat. The disguise had completely changed her appearance.

He looked beyond her to the path leading up to the cliff, but only saw a few trees. Anyone who ventured out here on this late night would be trespassing. He'd picked this secluded spot for that reason. "Were you seen?"

"Not that I know of," she said. "Though I doubt anyone would recognize me if they saw me."

A satisfied smile settled on his lips. "You're right about that."

Baggy clothes covered Julianna's feminine curves

and round breasts. A short, brown wig and America's Cup baseball cap hid her luxurious blond hair. With all the makeup scrubbed from her face, no one would mistake the fresh-faced kid for fashion icon Princess Julianna of Aliestle.

"You look like a teenager," he added.

"A teenage boy," she clarified. "You picked an excellent disguise for me."

She sounded appreciative, not upset. That surprised him a little. Most women wouldn't want to look like a boy. But then again, she hadn't wanted to get caught. A good disguise had been necessary.

"I had no problems, except Ortiz might want to reconsider his claim about no rats in the palace. I saw mice, and something...larger in the tunnel."

"Ortiz doesn't know about the tunnels. Only the royal family knows of their existence and an architect long dead," Alejandro explained. "The tunnels were built by pirates to hide treasure. When the king had them attached to the palace, a hand-selected crew was used. They were blindfolded and had no idea where they were working."

"How did the royal family find out about the tunnels?"

He grinned. "Supposedly my great-great-great grandfather was a king and pirate."

She laughed. The intoxicating sound floated on the air and made him want to inhale.

"You think that's funny."

"A little," she admitted. "But I'm not surprised you come from a line of pirates."

"Not a line," he clarified. "One pirate."

Amusement gleamed in her eyes. "If you say so."

"I do."

"Aye, aye, Captain," she teased.

It was his turn to laugh. Alejandro liked knowing he wasn't the only black sheep in his illustrious family line. He'd embraced the fact he had a pirate ancestor and thought others might, too. The island could capitalize on the colorful past except his father and brother didn't want the knowledge made public. "Ahoy, matey."

With an eager smile, she inspected *La Rueca* from bow to stern. "Lovely boat."

"I'm pleased with how she turned out." Alejandro touched the deck. He'd put everything he knew about boats and a fair share of money into her design. "Though she is untested in an actual race. The Med Cup will be interesting."

"You don't sound concerned."

"I'm not." If he were, he wouldn't have entered *La Rueca* in the race. "I'm confident she can perform and be competitive with the right wind and crew."

Julianna looked at the boat's name written in script on the stern. *"La Rueca."*

"The Spinning Wheel."

"Interesting name."

He stared at her slightly annoyed. "I already caved on the kitten. Are you going to challenge me on my boat's name, too?"

"No, but I'm curious if it has a special meaning."

"Most boat names do."

"What's the meaning behind yours?"

Alejandro remembered how persistent she'd been about the kitten's name. He had to tell her something. "*La Rueca* is a reminder that I haven't been spinning my wheels when it comes to boatbuilding."

"Spinning your wheels?" she asked.

Wanting to put an end to this topic of conversation, he lowered his one foot to the floor of the cockpit, reached back and started the outboard motor. He left it running in neutral. "Now is not the time."

"Later?"

"Do you always pester so much?"

"I'm sorry." Julianna raised her voice to talk over the idling motor. "Occupational hazard."

"Of being a princess?"

"Of having four younger brothers who never tell me anything unless I pester and pry. They are the only males, men, I'm allowed to be alone with for any extended period so they get the brunt of my curiosity." She looked around, not meeting his eyes. "Being out here with you like this…"

His annoyance disappeared. He appreciated her honesty. He also acknowledged the risk she was taking.

"It's okay. I'm not used to having a sister around." Though he didn't feel brotherly toward Julianna at all. "This is new for both of us."

She smiled softly. "I hope *La Rueca* turns out to be everything you wish for."

"Thanks. It's looking pretty good." And it was. A new sailboat design, a full moon and a beautiful woman to share a sail with tonight. She was so easy to talk to. He liked how she laughed.

Remember, sister-in-law. Julianna belonged with Enrique, not Alejandro. The realization left him feeling adrift.

Time to set a new course. They'd spent enough time talking. The longer they were out here, the more likely they were to be caught.

Alejandro extended his arm from the cockpit. "Climb aboard."

Julianna's hand clasped and melded with his. Heat shot up his arm. The reaction startled him, but he didn't let go. Truth was, he liked how her hand fit in his.

Her disguise might fool others, but not him. He knew she wasn't a teenager but a grown woman with lush, feminine curves. He'd held her in his arms and smelled the sweet fragrance of her shampoo. He wouldn't mind doing that again.

She stepped onto the boat and released his hand. As Alejandro flexed his fingers, she inhaled deeply. "I love the salty air."

"Wait until you get a taste of the sea spray."

"I'm looking forward to it." Gratitude shone in her eyes. "Thank you for going to so much trouble. Not many people would do this for a total stranger."

"It's my pleasure." And it was. Julianna looked so young, eager and pretty. Very, very pretty. "Besides you're not a stranger. You'll be family soon. My sister-in-law."

Alejandro said the words more for his benefit than hers. He waited for her to respond, but she didn't.

Julianna stared up at the clear, starry sky. The moonlight made her ivory complexion glow. Enrique didn't seem to understand the lovely princess from Aliestle. She was more than a showpiece, more than her dowry. She was a stunning, intelligent woman... Alejandro wondered why King Alaric had picked Enrique to be her husband. His brother had some admirable qualities, even if they disagreed over how best to help their country. But Julianna could do so much better.

"The weather is cooperating with us tonight." Her voice sounded lower, a little husky...sexy. Desire skimmed across his skin. "Lucky," she added.

Getting lucky tonight would be the perfect end to a midnight sail. Not that she would. Or he...

Yes, he would. The thought brought a lump of guilt to his throat.

"Let's get underway. I'll cast off." He motioned to the wheel. "Are you comfortable steering while we motor away from the dock?"

"Yes." She made her way toward the wheel. He moved out of her path, but her backside brushed him.

Heat burst through Alejandro. What the hell?

He didn't understand why he kept reacting to Julianna. She was his ticket to an independent life. He needed to control himself. A mistake could cost him his freedom from his father and the monarchy.

Some distance from Julianna would be good. Alejandro walked forward to the bow.

Maybe he should hit the clubs later tonight and connect with a pretty young thing. That would be the fastest way to get rid of whatever tension had built up and was stirring inside of him.

He pulled up a bumper, removed the bowline from the cleat and tossed the line onto the dock.

She stared up at the wind indicator. "Won't it look weird to be sailing at this hour?"

"No." He stepped over the lifeline, jumped onto the dock and moved to the aft section of the boat. "I always take out my new boats at night so people can't see the designs."

Julianna touched the wheel. "Sounds like boat-building is a competitive field."

"Everyone is looking for an edge." Alejandro pulled up the other bumper and unfastened the line from the boat's stern cleat. The rope fell to the dock. He stepped onto the boat with his left foot, shoved the boat away from the dock and hopped aboard with his right foot. "I'd rather they not steal mine."

"Confident."

"If I wasn't, I would crew on someone else's boat for the Med Cup. A boat that was a top contender."

Julianna reached back, shifted the motor to forward and twisted the throttle. She steered clear of the dock and headed out to open water. "Do you race a lot?"

"Not as much as I would like due to my royal obligations, but I hope that will change in the near future."

And it would. After Julianna married Enrique and they had a baby, Alejandro would have as much time as he wanted for business and sailing.

"Looks like there's a nice easy breeze tonight." She shot him an expectant look. "Ready for the mainsail."

It wasn't a question.

Interesting. She knew what to do without him saying a word. He hadn't expected that from her. Saying you enjoyed sailing while sipping a glass of wine and knowing what to do when you were on-board were two completely different things. Alejandro hadn't known what kind of sailor the princess was. So far, he was impressed by her knowledge. "I'll raise the main."

As he moved forward to the starboard side of the mast, she turned the boat head to wind.

Pointing the bow into the wind wasn't something instinctual. That took experience or good instruction. Whichever the case for Julianna, his respect increased.

"You know what you're doing out here." Alejandro yelled to be heard over the motor. He raised the mainsail with the halyard. "How long have you been sailing?"

"Since I was seven." She tailed the halyard and secured the line at the cleat on the top of the cabin. "My grandparents taught me how to sail on the Black Sea. Best vacation ever. How long have you sailed?"

"As long as I can remember." Alejandro shifted to the port side of the mast to hoist the jib, a triangular sail set forward of the main. He saw no other boats on the water. "Both my parents sail."

Julianna turned the wheel right to ease the bow starboard and trimmed the mainsail so it filled with the wind. The boat steadied and glided forward through the water. "I can't imagine anyone not sailing if they lived here."

The awe in her voice made him smile. "Me, neither."

She throttled down the motor, shifted to neutral and killed it.

The sudden quiet gave way to the sound of the hull cutting through the water and the breeze against the sails. Better get to it and make the most of the time they had out here.

Her sailing skills impressed him, but he wasn't going to assume what she knew or didn't know. "Ready for the jib."

She held the starboard sheet in her hand. One step ahead of him again. "Ready."

He hoisted the jib while she tailed the jib halyard. She secured the sheet by wrapping the rope around a cleat.

Alejandro moved aft to the cockpit. "Nice work."

With a wide smile, she gripped the wheel. "Thanks."

He gave her a compass heading.

Her eyes widened. "You want me to take the helm?"

She sounded like a teenager who'd been given the

keys to a brand-new car. He almost laughed. "You've got the wheel."

"I do, don't I?" Her grin was brighter than the full moon. She repeated the heading and turned toward the dock.

"Want to go back?" he asked.

As she shook her head, the cap didn't budge. "I want to make sure I have my bearings and know what the area looks like for our return."

Smart thinking. "You've sailed at night before."

"A few times, but I'd do the same thing if it were daytime."

His respect for her sailing abilities went up yet another notch. Alejandro trimmed the jib, adjusting the sheet to match her course and ensure the sail filled properly. Julianna adjusted the mainsail to match the heading.

He reached back and raised the motor out of the water. Now they would really move.

La Rueca accelerated through the water. Julianna kept her course, making minor corrections as she headed upwind. She seemed to have a feel for the boat as well as the wind.

"I love it out here." The look of pure joy on Julianna's face took Alejandro's breath away. "This is heaven. And you're an angel for doing this for me."

No angel. Not when he was getting turned on watching her sail. The gleam in her eyes. Her smiling lips. Her flushed cheeks.

He focused on the sails. They had filled perfectly, no trimming necessary.

"We're going to need to tack," she said.

He held onto the jib sheet. "Whenever you're ready."

"Tacking."

Alejandro bent over to avoid the boom as it swung across to the other side. The sails luffed, flapping in the wind. He pulled in the sheet. She trimmed the main.

Julianna sailed at a forty-five-degree angle to the wind.

The boat heeled. She leaned over the side to stare at the bow.

As the boat headed upwind, she tacked back and forth to keep the boat moving. With each direction change, the two of them worked together managing the sails with the sheets. Words weren't necessary. They both knew what to do. Perfectly in sync, like they'd done this a hundred times together. Alejandro continued to be amazed by Julianna's knowledge and skill.

He'd never seen someone with such a natural talent. She handled the boat as if it were an extension of herself. She seemed to know when the wind was going to change, and the perfect course to set to maximize the boat's speed.

With the wind on her face, she stared up at the full moon.

His heart lurched. She was truly stunning.

"This is even better than I imagined." Julianna's gaze met his. "Being out here on the sea like this... It's intoxicating."

He felt the same way being around her. "You steer like you've been sailing on the sea your entire life."

"Thanks," she said. "I love the way your boat responds."

"I love the way the boat responds to you." He wondered how she would respond to him, to his touch, to his kisses.

She eyed him curiously. "I'm sure she responds this way with any helmsman."

"Guess again," he admitted. "You handle *La Rueca* better than anyone else."

"Including you?"

"Yes."

She laughed. As before, the sweet sound carried on the wind. Alejandro wanted to reach out and capture it, a song to remind him of this perfect sail.

He wished the evening wouldn't have to end. As much as he'd like to keep Julianna out here all night, he couldn't. They'd sailed longer than he intended.

"Come about," he said. "And head downwind."

"Can't we head up a little farther?"

"It's time to go back." The disappointment in her eyes knotted his stomach. "You don't want to sneak into the palace when it's daylight. If your maid finds a blond wig and pillows in your bed…"

"That would be a disaster." Julianna gripped the wheel until her knuckles turned white. "Coming about."

The boat turned around. They sailed with the wind at their backs, running with the wind.

But Julianna no longer smiled. The sparkle disappeared from her eyes. She looked so...resigned.

Alejandro didn't like the change in her. Being out here on the water had set her free. The sailor with him tonight was the real Julianna. He didn't want her to put on a princess mask and have to wear it for the rest of her life. "Perhaps another time we can—"

"There can't be another time." She sounded dejected, sad. "This is my last sail. At least until Enrique changes his mind."

Her words echoed through his brain. He firmly rejected them. "I know it's forbidden and you can't risk being caught, but you're so happy out here."

"It's my fate."

Screw fate. Happiness was important, too.

Her last sail?

Not if Alejandro had any say in the matter.

CHAPTER SIX

WITH THE BOAT secured to the dock, Jules stood in the cockpit. She checked a sheet and wrapped it in a figure-eight pattern around a cleat. No way was the rope coming undone. Too bad her future couldn't be secured as easily.

The sail was over. With a sigh, she glanced at the bow. Soon she would be back in the palace. The thought squeezed her heart.

Below deck, Alejandro rummaged around, looking for a sail bag. Before long it would be time to go.

Emotion welled up inside her. She didn't want to return to reality yet. Nothing awaited her except a life of duty. Okay, she was being a total drama princess, but this once she would allow herself that luxury.

As the breeze picked up, the mast, standing so tall and strong, caught her attention. She closed her eyes and breathed in the salt air. The wind caressed her face. She could almost believe she was…free.

"Found it," Alejandro said from below.

Her eyelids flew open.

He climbed into the cockpit. "I need to organize the equipment."

"I'll do it for you now."

"It's too late."

Maybe for him. "I'll help you stow the sails."

"Good idea." Alejandro stood on the luff side of the mainsail. "We'll get out of here faster with two pairs of hands."

Her shoulders slumped. She should have offered to do the sails on her own. Getting out of here faster was the last thing she wanted.

She took the leech side. Together, they flaked the sail, layering the fabric across the boom. He secured the main with ties.

"What about the jib?" she asked.

He turned off the boat's running lights. "I'll take care of it when I get back."

Back? He was going out after this. To a club? The thought made her spirits sink lower. She should forget about it. Him. But she couldn't. "Where are you going?"

"I'm walking you back to the palace."

His chivalry pleased her, but she'd found her way to the dock on her own. She didn't need to be escorted back. A slow walk through the park on the way to the tunnels would keep her free a little while longer. Jules wanted as much extra time outside the palace as she could get. "I can find my own way."

"I know you can, but I'm going to escort you back."

"Okay." Jules caved like a house of cards. Truth was, she liked being with Alejandro and wanted to spend more time with him. Oh, she'd see him around the palace, at events and during meals. But given his relationship with Enrique, this might be their last chance to be alone.

She felt a pang in her heart.

The moonlight cast shadows on his face. With his strong jaw, nose and high cheekbones, he did look more pirate than prince. Too bad he wouldn't kidnap her, sail away with her on his boat and ravish her…

A smile tugged on the corners of her mouth. She couldn't help herself from daydreaming and fantasizing.

Alejandro was a hottie. He'd come to her rescue more than once. He might consider himself a black sheep, but black knight might be a better term after the sail tonight. He'd gone out of his way for her. Jules would be eternally grateful to him.

If only she could thank him, not with words, but a…kiss. A kiss would make tonight's sail more perfect. She stared at his full, soft-looking lips. A kiss under the full moon.

"Julianna?" Alejandro asked.

Desire flowed through her veins. "Yes?"

"You okay?"

"I'm just thinking." Of kissing him. All she had to do was rise up and touch her lips to his. Tempting, undeniably so. But the rebellious act of sailing was more than enough for the evening, for a lifetime really.

At least her lifetime. Jules took a deep breath.

"About our sail." She touched the boat's wheel, running her fingertips over the smooth edge. "I want to remember everything about tonight."

Everything except Alejandro.

Forget about kissing him. If she was to be Enrique's wife, she needed to bury all memories of Alejandro deep in her heart. Otherwise she would make herself and her marriage miserable, wanting what she couldn't have.

Not that Jules had real feelings for him or vice versa. They'd just met. She was getting carried away after a lovely evening with a fellow sailor. Alejandro hadn't flirted with her. He'd barely noticed her beyond her sailing abilities.

The setting with its full moon, starry sky and ocean breeze was perfect for two people to connect, to kiss. Yet he hadn't gotten caught up in the romantic atmosphere. That was a little…annoying. Maybe he didn't find her attractive.

What was she thinking? She shouldn't want him to hit on her.

"It's too bad we couldn't take pictures," he said.

"Yes." But having a photograph of tonight was too big a risk. If Enrique found it…

Enrique.

Maybe he was the reason Alejandro hadn't made a move on her. He might be the black sheep of the family, but he was an honorable man and not about to kiss his brother's fiancée.

She respected that. Respected him.

If only Enrique was more like his younger brother… Jules swallowed a sigh.

Alejandro double-checked the ties. "Ready to go?"

She took a final glance around. Everything had

been stowed or secured, but she was in no hurry to leave.

Waves lapped against the hull. The boat rocked with the incoming tide. The sound and motion comforted her. She ran her hand along the deck, a final farewell to *La Rueca*.

Regret mixed with sadness. "I'm ready."

She exited the boat without taking Alejandro's hand. She didn't need his help. Not anymore.

Touching him again, feeling her small hand clasped with his larger, warm one, would make putting tonight behind her harder. Being with him made her feel so different. She didn't know if that was freedom calling or not. But real life beckoned, or rather would with the sunrise.

Tears stung her eyes. Blinking them away, she headed up the dock. Her nonskid shoes barely made a sound against the wood.

Would the memory of tonight fade into nothingness as she embraced her role as Enrique's fiancée and wife? Jules hoped not.

She glanced up at the sky. A shooting star arced across the darkness.

I wish this didn't have to end.

The thought was instantaneous, and her entire body, from the top of her head to the tips of her toes, felt that way. She kept her gaze focused on the sky. The star and its tail vanished.

What a waste of a wish. Jules should have wished for Enrique to change his mind instead. She blew out a puff of air.

Time to stop pretending. She wasn't living a fairy tale, but it wasn't a Gothic novel, either. She needed to face up to her responsibilities.

Climbing the steep hillside, she ignored the burn in her thighs.

Alejandro caught up without sounding winded or breaking a sweat. He walked alongside her, shortening his stride to match hers. "I hope you enjoyed your sail."

"I did." She forced the words from her tight throat. Making small talk wasn't going to be easy. The walk back made her realize how prisoners at the Tower of London must have felt on their way to the executioner. Though Jules faced a life sentence, not death. A sentence she'd chosen for herself, for the sake of her brother, her children and her country. "Thank you so much for tonight."

"I should be the one thanking you."

Alejandro's easy smile doubled her heart rate. She wanted to scream and cry. If he'd been the first-born... No, a man like him would never need an arranged marriage to secure a bride. No matter what the amount of that bride's dowry.

"Watching you sail tonight has been a true pleasure, Julianna," he continued. "You're very skilled. Amazingly so."

His words made her stand taller. She needed to focus on the positives, not wallow in what-could-have-beens or what-ifs. "Plying me with compliments, huh?" she quipped.

"I'm telling you the truth."

The sincerity of his words lifted her burdened shoulders and lightened her heavy heart. "That means more to me than you can imagine."

His gaze locked with hers. Seconds turned into a minute. The way he looked into her eyes made her think he was going to kiss her. Jules wanted him to kiss her. Anticipation surged.

She leaned toward him and parted her lips. An invitation and a plea.

"You should be at the helm of *La Rueca* in the Med Cup," he said.

Her breath caught in her throat. "What did you say?"

He repeated the words.

A strong yearning welled up inside of her, a longing that didn't want to be ignored. She started to speak then stopped herself.

What he said was impossible. In fact, he looked as surprised at his words as Jules did. He must have been joking.

She pushed aside her disappointment and laughed. "Oh, yes. That's exactly what I should do. Princess Julianna of Aliestle, helmsman."

Alejandro didn't joke back. His smile disappeared. His eyes darkened.

"You're not laughing," she said.

His jaw thrust forward. "I'm not kidding."

Of course, he was. Jules reached the top of the hill continued along the paved path through the park. been a lovely evening. Please don't spoil it by ng me."

"I'm serious." The determined set of his chin made him look formidable. A lot like his father. But she remained unnerved by that. "If *La Rueca* places in the top five, the resulting publicity will boost my boatyard's reputation and raise the island's standing in the eyes of the yachting world. To do that I need you steering the boat."

"Wait." What he said confused her. "You said you were confident in the boat. In your crew."

"That was before I saw you sail. I need you, Julianna."

His words smacked into her like an unwieldy suitcase on wheels a porter couldn't handle and nearly knocked her on her backside. No one had ever needed her before.

"I'm floored. Flabbergasted. Flattered." Jules bit her lip to stop from rambling. She needed to be sensible about this, not emotional. "But we both know I can't race with you. The Med Cup is right before the wedding. Enrique and my father are unlikely to change their minds and allow me to compete, even with you."

"This will be our secret."

Jules considered what he was saying…for a nano-second. "That's…that's…"

"Doable."

"Insane," she countered. "If I get caught—"

"We'll make sure you aren't."

A mix of conflicting emotion battled inside Jul Part of her wanted to grab the moment and make most of the opportunity. But common sense kep feet planted firmly on the ground, er, path. She forced herself to keep walking toward the grotto.

"We're not talking about a midnight sail with the two of us. I'd have to practice with a crew in daylight. They'd figure out I'm not a boy the first time I said anything." Coming up with a list of reasons this was a bad idea was too easy. "Let's not forget the race officials. A crew roster will be necessary. We can't overlook the media coverage. The press will have a field day if my identity is discovered."

"For someone who's never sailed on the ocean you sure know a lot about what's involved with racing."

"I've raced in lakes, and I've followed various racing circuits for years. I know enough…" Her voice raised an octave. She took a calming breath. It didn't help. "Enough to know that with me at the helm, the odds are you'll lose. I'm not experienced enough."

"Are you trying to convince me?" he asked. "Or yourself."

"You."

"I say you're qualified enough. I want you to be my helmsman."

She felt as if she'd entered a different dimension, an alternative universe. Perhaps this was a dream and La Isla de la Aurora didn't exist. She would wake up in her room at the castle in Aliestle, not engaged. "Consider what you're saying, Alejandro. You're crazy if you want to risk the Med Cup on someone like me."

"Maybe I'm crazy. Certifiably insane. But I know

what I saw tonight out on the water. No one else handles *La Rueca* as well as you."

"Have them practice more," she said. "It's late. I must get back to the palace before the sun rises."

She quickened her pace, leaving Alejandro behind. The sooner she reached the grotto, the better. She couldn't listen to him anymore. It hurt too much to think racing on the ocean was even a possibility. That had never crossed her mind given her father's restrictions.

The footsteps behind her drew closer. "Don't run away."

"I'm heading in the wrong direction if I wanted to do that."

"Stop."

Jules did. She owed him that much for tonight's sail.

He placed his hand on her shoulder.

She gasped, not expecting him to touch her.

"Please," he said. "Consider what I'm saying."

Warmth ebbed from the point of contact. She struggled against the urge to lean into him, to soak up his strength and confidence. She wanted to, but couldn't. She shrugged away from his hand and counted to twenty in French. "I've considered it. No."

"Racing will make you happy." He wasn't giving up for some reason. "You love to sail."

"I love to sail, but it isn't my entire life." Jules didn't dare look at Alejandro. She couldn't allow herself to be swayed, even if she was tempted. "I have a duty to my family and country. That is more important than some…hobby."

The word used derisively by her father tasted bitter on her tongue. Sailing was a pastime, but it represented the freedom to live as she wanted and a tangible connection to the mother she didn't remember.

"I can't risk upsetting Enrique." The reality of her situation couldn't be ignored. "If he finds out—"

"Do you really think Enrique's going to send you back to Aliestle and walk away from a hundred-million-dollar dowry because you went sailing?"

Her jaw dropped. So did her heart. *Splat.*

Jules knew her father had set aside a large amount of money for her dowry, but not *that* much. She closed her mouth. She'd always known suitors were after the money, not her. Still the truth stung. "I…can't."

"Yes, you can," he urged. "It'll be worth the risk."

"For you, maybe. Not for me." If Enrique didn't marry her, she'd find herself trapped in a worse marriage, in an old-fashioned country with archaic, suffocating traditions. Her efforts to help Brandt and Aliestle would be futile. Plus, she had her children to consider. "I would love to race. But I can't do all the things I want to do. I must consider the consequences."

"Consider the consequences if you don't race."

The word *no* sat on the tip of Jules's tongue. That word would end further discussion. But her heart wasn't ready to do that yet. She wanted to know what racing might feel like. But reality kept poking at her, reminding her what was at stake. "There are no consequences if I don't race."

Alejandro held her hand. "Your happiness, Julianna."

"I'll find happiness."

"Life on the island will be good for you, but Enrique is self-involved. He'll most likely ignore you."

"Ignoring me will be better than trying to control me," she admitted. "And I'll be happy once I have children. I've always wanted to be a mother. Children will bring me great happiness and joy. I'll devote myself to being the best mother I can be. That will make me very happy."

"Will children be enough?"

They had to be.

"I'm sorry, Alejandro." Julianna pulled her hand out of his. "I must find contentment in the life I'm meant to live. If I believe I can or should have more, that will make the days unbearable."

"You're a wonderful, brave woman."

"If I was brave, I'd say yes even though it would be a really bad idea."

"It could be sheer brilliance."

"Or an utter disaster."

"You want to." Alejandro gazed into her eyes. "I can tell."

Her pulse skittered. She flushed. She did want to. More than anything. "I told you. It doesn't matter what I want. I can't."

"What's really stopping you?"

"Common sense." She raised her hand in the air to accentuate each point. "Duty. Obligation."

"Royal duty doesn't mean making yourself a slave."

"It's not slavery, but a responsibility to build something better."

"I'm trying to build something better here on the island. But you can't pretend to be something you're not," Alejandro said. "However much we love people or have loved them, we still have to be the person we are meant to be. Follow your heart," his voice dipped, low and hypnotic.

Emotion clogged her throat. She'd followed her heart once. Tonight. The thought of doing so again made her mouth water. "I…"

"Say yes," he encouraged. "You won't regret racing."

Oh, she would regret it. Jules had no doubt.

But tonight's glimpse of freedom had spoiled her and made her feel carefree and alive. She wasn't ready for that feeling to end.

"Yes." Her answer went against everything she'd been raised to do or be. She needed to reel herself in and set clear boundaries to temper this recklessness. She remembered her plan from this morning. "I'm saying yes for the same reason I sailed tonight. Once I marry Enrique, things will change. I must honor my husband and my marriage. I will step fully into my role of the crown princess who will one day be queen."

"The people of La Isla de la Aurora have no idea how fortunate they are to have you as their future queen."

"Let's make sure I'm not caught so one day I *can* be their queen."

"That's the number one priority," Alejandro said. "I'll take every precaution to keep your identity a secret. I have as much to lose with this as you do."

His words didn't make any sense. This had nothing to do with him. "What do you mean?"

Alejandro hesitated.

"I want to know what you have to lose," she said.

"My freedom," he admitted. "Once you and Enrique marry and have children, I'll be free from all royal obligations. I can concentrate on business and not have to worry about any more princely duties."

Enrique had said Alejandro didn't want to be royalty anymore. She'd thought Enrique had been exaggerating. Maybe that was what Alejandro had meant about being the person he needed to be. "You really want to turn your back on all your duties?"

"Yes."

She admired his being true to himself while dealing with some of the same burdens she had as a royal, but his wanting to break off completely from his obligations and birthright saddened her. Yet she had to admit, she was a tad envious. Alejandro would sail off into the sunset and do what he wanted, whereas she would carry the weight of two countries' expectations on her shoulders for the rest of her life.

At least she knew he would do everything in his power to keep them from getting caught. "I guess we both have something to lose."

"We're in this together, Julianna."

Yes, they were, but the knowledge left her feeling unsettled. Being out here alone with him did, too. His nearness disturbed her. His lips captured her attention. She still felt an overwhelming urge to kiss him. Even if he was the last man she should kiss.

Keep walking. Julianna saw the grotto up ahead. "We'd better get into the tunnel before someone sees us out here."

"No one will see us." Alejandro spoke with confidence. "I own this place."

"What place?"

He motioned to the land surrounding them. "The dock. The park. Everything you see."

She tried to reconcile this new piece of information with what she knew about him. Enrique had made Alejandro sound as if only sailing mattered to him. "You're a boatbuilder and a real estate investor?"

He nodded. "My goal is to turn the island into a travel hotspot. Most of the tourist traffic goes to other islands along the coast of Spain. La Isla de la Aurora doesn't have enough quality hotels, resorts and marinas to attract the big spenders. My father and brother have a more low-key vision of how to improve the economy. But the Med Cup has helped attract the yachting crowd. Now I have to get the travel industry onboard."

Impressive. And unexpected. He was so much more than she'd originally thought. Not that anything he owned or said or did should matter to her.

But it did. A lot.

She chewed on the inside of her cheek.

"As I mentioned, *La Rueca*'s result in the Med Cup could help that happen sooner," he said. "If we finish well."

We. The realization of what she'd agreed to hit her full force. Pressure to do well. Practice time. Being with Alejandro, a man she was attracted to. One who would be related to her when they finished racing. Oh, what a tangled web she was weaving. No way would she be able to escape unscathed.

"This isn't going to work." Doubts slammed into her like a rogue wave. "Someone at the palace will notice I'm not around if we have to practice a lot."

"Don't worry." He tucked a stray strand of blond hair up into the wig and adjusted the cap on her head. "I'll figure everything out. Trust me."

Jules shivered with desire and apprehension. She would have to trust him in a way she'd never trusted anyone before.

"Do you really think we have a shot at doing well?" she asked.

One side of his mouth tipped up at the corner. "With you at the helm, we have a good shot at not only placing, but winning."

CHAPTER SEVEN

THE SOUND OF voices woke Julianna. Lying in bed, she blinked open her eyes. Morning already. The bright sunlight made her shut her eyes again. But she'd glimpsed enough to know this wasn't her room back in Aliestle. She hadn't been dreaming.

Last night had been real. The sail. Alejandro.

A shiver ran down her spine.

She'd agreed to race, to be on his crew.

Somehow, she would have to be Enrique's conventional princess-fiancée and Alejandro's helmsman. And not let the two roles collide. Her temples throbbed thinking about trying to negotiate between the two different worlds without anyone figuring out what she was doing.

"The princess is sleeping, sir." Yvette's voice became more forceful. "I don't want to wake her unless it's necessary."

"This is important," a male voice Jules recognized as Brandt's said.

She opened her eyes and raised herself up on her elbows.

Yvette wore the traditional castle housekeeper

uniform—a black dress with white collar and apron. Her brown hair was braided and rolled into a tight bun. She had the door cracked and held onto it with white knuckles, as if to keep an intruder out. Jules pictured Brandt standing on the other side, trying to sway the young maid with a flirtatious smile.

"I'm awake, Yvette," Jules said. "Send Brandt in."

"The princess is no longer sleeping, sir." Yvette opened the door all the way. "You may come in."

Brandt strode in, looking every inch the crown prince in his navy suit, striped dress shirt and colorful tie. He laughed. "I was out clubbing most of the night yet you're the one in bed. Must have been an exciting night watching TV?"

Jules shrugged. The night had been more exciting than she imagined. She hadn't been able to fall asleep when she'd returned to the palace. Too many thoughts about Alejandro had been running through her brain. Each time she closed her eyes, she'd seen his handsome face, as if the features had been etched in her memory.

She watched her maid head into the bathroom. "What is so important?"

"Prince Enrique wants you downstairs now."

Jules glanced at the clock. A quarter past ten. "Nothing is listed on my schedule."

If so, Yvette would have never allowed her to sleep in. The maid always made sure Jules was ready on time for her scheduled events.

Brandt raised a brow. "It's a surprise."

Her brother sounded amused. That set off warning bells in her head. "Care to enlighten me about this surprise?"

"No."

She tossed one of her pillows at him.

He batted it away. "Hey, don't shoot the messenger. I'm only doing as requested. I assumed you'd rather have me wake you than Enrique."

Alejandro would have been better. Especially if he woke her with long, slow kisses... She pushed the thought away as she fought a blush. Steering the boat was her responsibility, not kissing him. "I'll get dressed."

Brandt held up his hand as if to stop her. "That won't be necessary."

She drew back. "Excuse me?"

Mischief filled his eyes. "Enrique said a robe and slippers are fine."

She made a face. "I don't like the sound of this."

"No worries," Brandt said. "Bring Yvette. She and I will ensure your reputation isn't sullied."

If Jules had been caught last night, her reputation would have been more than sullied. "You've been spending too much time with Father. It's influencing your vocabulary."

"I happen to like sullying young maidens."

She rolled her eyes. "Give me five minutes. I'll meet you in the hallway."

"Don't take any longer," he cautioned. "Enrique said this is important."

Worry shivered down her spine. Had Enrique

found out about last night? But if that were the case, why wouldn't he want her to dress before coming downstairs?

Brandt strode out of the room and closed the door behind him.

Jules slid out from under the covers and stood on the rug. Her simple white nightgown looked nothing like what a stylish princess would wear to bed. Her father forbade her to wear any sort of pajamas that were too pretty or feminine because she wasn't married. Forget sexy lingerie. She felt lucky wearing underwire bras decorated with lace. The castle's head housekeeper confiscated purchases she deemed inappropriate by King Alaric's standards.

Yvette returned, holding a lavender-colored, terrycloth robe and matching slippers. "ma'am."

"I'd rather dress."

"I don't think there is time, ma'am."

Jules heard the sympathy in Yvette's voice. "Do you have any idea what's going on downstairs?"

"No, Ma'am." Yvette helped her into the thick robe. "But people have been arriving at the palace since early this morning. I'm surprised the noise didn't wake you."

Jules had been dead to the world once she'd quieted her thoughts of Alejandro and fallen asleep. She couldn't remember the last time she'd slept so soundly. She didn't remember any of her dreams. A rarity for her. "I didn't hear a thing."

"You must have been tired, ma'am."

She nodded.

Lines creased Yvette's forehead. "Are you feeling well, ma'am? Should I request a doctor be sent to the palace?"

"No worries, Yvette," Jules said. "I'm not sick. Let's go see what Enrique's surprise is all about."

Something good, she hoped. And something that had nothing to do with last night.

Alejandro stared at the attractive, stylish women carrying boxes into the palace's large music room. These weren't members of the normal staff. Not with those long legs and short skirts. His curiosity piqued, he decided to take a closer look and entered the Grand Hall.

Enrique paced with his hands clasped behind his back. Wrinkles creased his forehead. Sweat beaded at his brow. The crown prince looked nothing like the oil paintings of the island's rulers hanging on the walls alongside him.

But Alejandro had seen his brother this way once before, when he prepared for what would turn out to be a disastrous date with a famous movie actress. The spoiled, pampered, egotistical couple had clashed from the moment they said hello. Each expected the other to cater to their whims.

"What are you up to, bro?" Alejandro asked.

"I wondered when the scent of perfume would lead you here." Enrique dabbed his forehead with a linen handkerchief. "Look, but don't touch. The women are being paid handsomely for their services."

Alejandro raised a brow. "I didn't realize you paid for female services."

"Not those kind of services, moron." Enrique sneered. "This is a surprise for Julianna."

"A surprise. Really?"

"Don't sound so shocked." He continued pacing. "She is going to be my wife."

Alejandro wasn't about to forget about that. He'd resisted tasting her lips last night for that very reason. But her agreeing to be his helmsman made up for the lack of kisses.

Asking her to join his crew wasn't his smartest move given consequences involved, but he believed *La Rueca* had a better chance of winning with her behind the wheel. She'd also looked so happy sailing. He wanted to show her how beautiful life could be here. All he had to do was douse his attraction for her, and things would be fine.

"I know." He tried to sound nonchalant, even if he was a little…envious. Enrique hadn't had much luck in the dating department, but he'd hit the jackpot finding a bride. Not that Alejandro was in the market for one himself. "But you've never gone to so much trouble for a woman before."

Any trouble, really. Enrique expected women to fall at his feet. Those with dreams of being a princess and queen would until they tired of his self-centeredness. But Julianna was different…

"The royal wedding will generate a tremendous amount of publicity." He lowered his voice. "Julianna must be dressed appropriately for the ceremony and reception."

Too bad Enrique needed to feed his ego, not please Julianna the way she deserved to be pleased and cherished. Alejandro rolled his eyes in disgust.

"The princess is always at the top of the Best Dressed Lists." He hadn't been able to sleep last night. He'd searched the internet to learn more about Julianna. "She is a fashion icon for women, young and old."

"In everyday clothing, yes," Enrique said. "Being a princess bride is different. I have assembled the top experts here. A dress designer and her team, makeup artists, hairstylists and many others. This is all for her."

Alejandro rolled his eyes. "Don't pretend any of this is for Julianna. It's about how you want her to look when she's with you."

"This is important. The royal wedding will change the island's fortune and future. Everything must go perfectly." Enrique sounded more like a spoiled child than a crown prince. "Today's trial run of our wedding day preparations will work out any kinks and problems. The dress designer will also take care of alterations needed on the wedding gown."

Practical, perhaps, but so not romantic. Julianna was practical. Her words last night about her embracing her marriage told Alejandro that. But the woman who had sailed with stars in her eyes also seemed like the kind who liked the hearts, flowers and violin type of romance. Arranged marriage or not.

"Alterations?" he asked. "I didn't think Julianna had a wedding dress yet."

Enrique smirked. "She has one now."

The look on his brother's face worried Alejandro. "What have you—?"

"Good morning, gentlemen." Julianna walked toward them with Brandt at her side and her maid following.

Julianna looked regal wearing a bathrobe and slippers. Every strand of her hair, worn loose this morning, was perfectly placed. She'd applied makeup, too. Not as much as she usually wore, but enough for him to notice the difference from her clean face last night. No one would guess the perfectly groomed princess had another side, one that had taken her out onto the sea with him until early this morning.

She stopped in front of them. "I was told you wanted to see me, Enrique."

Her formal tone contradicted the casual way she'd spoken on the boat and during the walk back to the palace.

"I do." Enrique beamed. "I have a surprise for you, my lovely bride."

The corners of her mouth tipped up, but her eyes didn't sparkle the way they had last night. Of course, no one would notice that except Alejandro. He found it strange she showed no hint of the woman he'd spent hours sailing with. Her mask was firmly in place, a disguise like the sailing clothes she'd worn.

Julianna rubbed her hands together. Excited or cold, he couldn't tell. "I love surprises," she said.

Alejandro didn't think she would like this one. She wanted freedom, not be told what to wear and how to act on her wedding day. He needed to warn her so she would be prepared. "Why don't you grab Father, Enrique? I'm sure he'll be interested in seeing this."

"Father is attending his weekly breakfast meeting with the head of the Courts. Something you would know if you had a clue about what went on around here." Enrique extended his arm, and Julianna laced her arm around his. "Ready for your surprise?"

She nodded with a hint of anticipation in her eyes.

The woman always hoped for the best. Alejandro respected that about her, but he knew she would only be hurt that much more.

The doors to the music room opened.

Alejandro stared at the floor. He didn't want to see her disappointed.

Julianna gasped.

His gaze jerked up. White satin, tulle and miniature white lights covered the walls of the music room. A thick, white rug lay on the hardwood floor. A white silk curtain separated a third of the room from the rest of it. No expense had been spared in transforming the space into a spa complete with a private beauty salon and a massage table.

Impressive. Enrique had managed to get it right this time. If only his motivation had been for his bride and not himself. Alejandro glanced over at Julianna.

She surveyed the entire room with wide-eyed wonder. "What is all this?"

"Everything you'll need to prepare for our wedding day," Enrique said proudly. "This will be your bride room."

"Oh, Enrique." Her smile widened. "I can't believe you would go to all this trouble."

Don't believe it, Alejandro wanted to shout. This was nothing but smoke and mirrors on the part of his brother. Ambition and pride run amuck à la Lady Macbeth. But Alejandro saw how moved Julianna was. He wanted her to be happy, even if that meant she was happy with his brother. Enrique might get Julianna the princess, but Alejandro took fierce delight in getting Julianna the sailor.

"This is amazing, Enrique," Brandt said. "Thank you so much."

Even Brandt had been fooled.

Enrique kissed the top of Julianna's hand, the gesture as meaningless as the over-the-top display in the music room.

"It was no trouble at all." Enrique's smooth tone made Alejandro want to gag. "Anything for my princess bride."

Julianna's eyes didn't sparkle, but they brightened. She looked relieved, pleased with what she saw in the music room and with her fiancé. "Thank you."

Warmth and appreciation rang out in her voice. Perhaps she would be content, even happy, in this marriage. But Alejandro couldn't shake his misgivings.

Enrique's chest puffed out. "There's more."

Alejandro had to admit he was curious, but in a train-wreck-waiting-to-happen kind of way.

With a grand gesture of his arms, Enrique motioned for the curtain to be opened. Two young women, both dressed in the same hot pink above the knee dresses and black sling-back stilettos, opened the white silk curtains to reveal a wedding gown on a busty mannequin wearing a diamond tiara and a long lace veil.

"Surprise," Enrique shouted with glee.

Julianna gasped again. Not in a good way this time. A look of despair flashed across her face before her features settled into a tight smile.

Alejandro didn't blame her for the reaction.

A cupcake. That was his first impression of the gown. The frilly dress with big puffy sleeves, sparkling crystals and neatly tied bows would look perfect on a Disney princess, but not on Julianna. She would look like a caricature of a princess bride in that dress.

Julianna should wear a more sophisticated, elegant gown with sleek lines to show off her delicious curves. He imagined her walking down the cathedral aisle in such a dress and pictured himself waiting for her...

What the hell?

Alejandro shook the image from his head. He wasn't looking for a girlfriend, let alone a bride. Especially one who was already engaged and held the key to his freedom.

Julianna stared at the spectacle of a dress in front of her. Tears welled in her eyes.

"I told you she would like this." A smug smile settled on Enrique's lips. "She's crying tears of joy."

Alejandro balled his hands. He barely managed to keep his fists at his sides. He wanted to punch his brother in the nose and knock some sense into his inflated, ego-filled head.

The guy had to be a narcissist not to realize Julianna was horrified, not joyful. Either that, or Enrique was that dense about women.

"That is my sister's wedding dress?" Brandt asked with a tone of disbelief.

Enrique nodded, visibly pleased with himself. "I told the designer to create a royal wedding dress fit for a fairy-tale princess bride."

"When?" Julianna muttered. "When did you tell her that?"

"A while ago," Enrique admitted. "When my father decided I should wed."

Julianna pressed her lips together. Alejandro didn't have to be a mind reader to know what she was thinking. Enrique had requested the gown for a generic bride, not with Julianna in mind.

More proof this show today was for Enrique's benefit, no one else's. He knew exactly how *he* wanted things. Who cared about anyone else, including his bride who hadn't even been considered in the dress design?

Alejandro had come up against his brother's ego many times. He'd lost most battles and won a few, but he'd never been so angry with Enrique as he was now.

"Try on the dress," Enrique urged.

Alejandro waited for Julianna to speak up, to say she wanted to pick out her own wedding dress.

She squared her shoulders.

He smiled. This should be good.

"Let's go see how the dress looks on me, Yvette." Julianna set off toward the wedding dress with her maid in tow.

Alejandro stared in disbelief. Julianna had no problem yesterday speaking up to him, showing sass and spunk when it came to Boots's name and being helmsman. He couldn't understand why she remained silent now.

He glanced at Brandt. Surely the crown prince would stand up for his big sister? But he followed Julianna without saying a word.

What was going on? Alejandro watched from the other side of the music room as they approached the atrocious wedding gown.

"I knew this was a good idea," Enrique said in a low, but singsong manner.

Alejandro gritted this teeth. "A bride should choose her own gown."

"This was part of the wedding negotiations with King Alaric."

"The king approves of Julianna wearing a dress you picked out?" Alejandro asked.

Enrique nodded. "King Alaric paid for all of this, including the wedding gown I commissioned months ago. The old fool is so desperate to have grandchildren he agrees to anything I ask for. He's giving me an extra ten million if I keep Julianna from ever sailing again. Imagine that."

"I can't." Outrage tightened Alejandro's jaw until it ached. For that amount of money, Enrique would never change his mind about Julianna sailing again. "Especially since she seems to enjoy the sport."

"She'll get over it." Enrique's brush-off bothered Alejandro more than usual. "Remember, she has me. That will be enough for her."

His brother's uncaring attitude roused Alejandro's protective instincts. Someone had to take a stand for her. "Julianna might be happier if—"

Enrique cut him off. "Her happiness isn't my priority. I only care about her dowry, ability to produce heirs and obeying my orders."

Alejandro had never seen his brother act so callous. "This is wrong."

"I'm treating her the way she expects to be treated. Women in Aliestle are used to being ordered about. It's all they know."

"Enrique, don't—"

"Enough." Enrique sneered. "If you say a word to Julianna or Brandt about any of this, I'll shut down the Med Cup this year."

"You can't cancel the race."

"I can, and I will."

With the threat hanging in air, he strutted toward the others like a proud peacock.

Alejandro seethed. He needed his brother to marry if he wanted to be released from his princely duties and obligations. But what would the cost of that freedom be?

He stared at Julianna. She touched the skirt of the wedding dress with a hesitant hand. She claimed marrying Enrique was better than returning to Aliestle. Alejandro had his doubts.

The women in pink removed the frothy confection of a wedding gown from the mannequin. Julianna and her maid followed them behind a white, fabric-paneled screen.

Enrique's threat made it impossible for Alejandro to take action. Not that he could stop the royal wedding since Julianna wanted to marry his brother. But Alejandro could do something else.

He could make the Med Cup race memorable for Julianna. He could show her how skilled and talented she was. He could make her see she deserved the best from the crew, the staff and most especially, her husband.

That was the least Alejandro could do for the beautiful princess bride. And he would.

I look like a puff pastry.

Jules stared at her reflection in the three-part mirror with horror. She couldn't believe Enrique wanted her to wear this monstrosity at their wedding. She'd thought for a few short moments he'd wanted to make her happy and gone to all this trouble to make her feel…special. But he hadn't.

Do you really think Enrique's going to send you

back to Aliestle and walk away from a hundred-million-dollar dowry because you went sailing?

Alejandro's words reaffirmed what she knew in her heart and her mind. Enrique only cared about her dowry. He'd made it sound like all this had been for her, but it was really for him. She'd overheard the manicurist talking to the hairstylist about putting together a list of improvements for the crown prince. No one cared about Jules's opinion.

Thank goodness Enrique hadn't stuck around long. Otherwise she might have said something impolite. At least she didn't feel quite so guilty about agreeing to sail in the Med Cup and going behind his back.

One of the women in pink raised the hem of the dress. Tulle scratched Jules leg. "We'll need to add another ruffle."

No. Her stomach churned. Not another ruffle. The dress had too many as it was.

She inhaled to calm herself. The potent mixture of the different perfumes the women wore made her cough. Her eyes watered.

Delia, the dress designer, and her team jotted notes and marked the dress with pins.

Jules tried to ignore them. She needed a distraction. A quick survey of the room yielded nothing. Alejandro must have left before Enrique. She would have to rely on her own imagination.

She imagined being on *La Rueca* and holding the wheel in her hands. The metal felt smooth beneath her palms. The boat heeled and water splashed against her face and wet her clothes. Alejandro manned the jib sheet, his flexed muscles glistening from a combination of sweat and water. He glanced back at her. His handsome face filled with pleasure, his dark eyes gleaming with hunger for her. An answering desire sparked low in her belly as the wind whipped through her hair—

"With the dreamy look in your eyes, you must be picturing your wedding day," a woman's voice broke through Julianna's thoughts.

She turned off the romantic scene playing in her head and brought herself back to the present.

"You look gorgeous, ma'am." Delia motioned to the women in pink. "Let's button up the back to see how the gown fits."

Jules didn't—couldn't—say anything. She'd rather daydream about sailing with Alejandro than think about marrying a man who would have a wedding gown designed for a nameless, faceless bride. A dress more suited for a younger woman who wanted to be a fairy-tale princess, not a woman a couple of years away from turning thirty. The thought of walking down the aisle wearing the dress filled her with dread.

Don't think about that. She imagined herself with the wind on her face, the taste of salt in her mouth and Alejandro next to her.

Someone pulled on the left side of dress. "It's a little tight."

Jules pretended the lifeline tugged against her, keeping her attached to the boat. With iffy weather and big waves, falling overboard could be fatal.

As would be continuing to fantasize about Alejandro.

"It'll fit," another woman said.

The pressure around Jules's midsection increased. She felt as if she were caught in the middle of a tug-of-war game. The air rushed from her lungs, forced out by whatever was being tightened around her.

"Can't breathe," Jules croaked.

"Release the buttons and strings," Delia ordered.

The women did.

"Thank you," Jules said.

"Sorry, Ma'am." Delia's cheeks flushed. "The dress is too large in the bust and too small in the waist. I'll take measurements so I can alter the gown."

Enrique must have given the measurements for his idea of the perfect bride. Jules wasn't surprised he wanted an eighteen-year-old woman with the proportions of a real-life Barbie doll. She remembered the room he'd picked out for her with the garden view to make her happy. One of Enrique's problems was he assumed everyone's tastes were the same as his own or should be.

Using a measuring tape, the designer and her assistants took measurements and scribbled notes.

Jules wanted to laugh at the absurdity of it all, but despair crept along the edges of her mind, threatening to swamp her. The reality of what kind of marriage she would have had become clearer.

Running away, giving up duty and family for happiness, no longer seemed like such a drastic measure. She could shuck the awful dress and flee. No more grinning and bearing it. No more doing what everyone else wanted her to do.

But that behavior wasn't any more her than the wedding gown. Jules wanted a better future for her children and her country. She had a plan. She would have to be content with her sailing rebellion.

"That is all we need, Ma'am," Delia said. "I'll start to work on the alterations right away. I shall also remove some of the bows and layers. Prince Enrique talked about a fairy-tale princess dress. That led me to believe you were younger. My mistake."

"You've worked hard on the dress, Delia. The craftsmanship and quality are outstanding. I know you've delivered the wedding dress Prince Enrique asked for," Jules said. "But I'm twenty-eight. Not eighteen. Anything you can do to make the gown a little more…subdued would be appreciated."

Delia bowed her head. "I understand, ma'am."

The woman's empathetic tone told Jules the designer understood. Was that enough to make up for her having to wear the dress and marry an egotistical crown prince? She exhaled on a sigh.

Enrique was to be her husband. She had to make the best of the situation and the most of the opportunity. Jules straightened. "So where am I to go next?"

"The massage table, ma'am." Yvette read from a sheet of paper. "Then you're to have a pedicure and manicure before seeing the hairstylist and makeup artist."

"I'll be all made up with nowhere to go," she said, trying to sound lighthearted and cheerful.

"You do have someplace to go, ma'am." Yvette waved a piece paper. "I received an updated itinerary for today. You, Prince Brandt and the royal family are attending the ballet tonight."

Jules hoped that included Alejandro. Her heart bumped. The thought of seeing him again—make that racing with him—was the only thing keeping her going right now.

Thank goodness she'd said yes to being his helmsman or she didn't know what she would do. The memory of racing would keep her going until she had children to love.

Maybe she would get pregnant right away.

On her wedding night.

With Enrique.

The thought of being intimate with him seared her heart. Tears stung the corners of her eyes. She looked up at the elaborate crystal chandelier hanging from the ceiling and blinked. Twice.

Jules knew better than to let her emotions show. She'd been trained from a young age to hide her true feelings. She had to be more careful or someone might discover the truth about how she felt.

Shoulders back. Chin up. Smile.

She looked at Yvette. "So, which ballet will I be seeing?"

CHAPTER EIGHT

THE SUN HAD yet to peek over the horizon. As Jules made the early morning trek to Alejandro's boat dock, her headlamp illuminated the way through the darkness. The scent of cut grass hung in the air. The smell was new, different from the night before. Someone must have mowed yesterday. Or maybe she was paying closer attention this time.

Knowing where she was going made the walk easier. But the stillness was a little eerie. Even the insects seemed to have called it a night. If only she had gotten more sleep...

Jules yawned.

The four-hour ballet and the dessert afterward had dragged on into the wee hours of the night. She'd slept for three hours before having to wake and prepare for this practice. She felt half-asleep.

Too bad the Lilac Fairy from the ballet couldn't lead a handsome prince to Jules. A kiss might wake her up, especially if the kiss came from a certain prince.

Alejandro.

Warmth balled in her chest.

He'd been at the ballet for the first act, long enough to slip a note about this morning's practice into Jules's beaded clutch. He'd left the royal family's private box before the start of the first intermission, well before the kissing happened in act two. She'd been sad to see him go. Not for any other reason than she enjoyed his company, she decided.

Jules knew she would never be anything more than Alejandro's sister-in-law. Anything more would be wrong. But she allowed herself the luxury of day-dreaming about him until her wedding day. A guilty pleasure, yes. But a necessary one if she wanted to make it through her engagement without losing her mind.

Jules wanted to like her future husband. She wanted to fall in love with him. But he wasn't making it easy. He'd paraded her around like a puppet bride on a string during both intermissions. Enrique didn't want a wife; he wanted a fashion accessory.

She shivered with disgust at the way he'd showed her off and talked about her as if she weren't there. At least he hadn't tried to kiss her good-night.

Forget about it. Him. She needed to focus on sailing.

But Jules couldn't muster the same level of enthu-siasm she'd felt venturing out here yesterday. Partly because of what had happened with Enrique, but also because she would be meeting the crew for the first. She wouldn't be Julianna, but J.V., a nineteen-year-old male university student from Germany who knew enough English sailing commands to be an effective helmsman.

Jules wore the same disguise as before, but she didn't know if she could pull off her new identity. The waist of her pants slipped down her hips. She pulled the pants up and rolled the band. Maybe that would make it fit better.

A wave of apprehension swept over her.

Alejandro thought she could do it, but the man exuded confidence. He thought he could do anything. He seemed to believe the same of her, too. Jules wished she was as certain, but all she felt were... misgivings.

At the top of the hill, she stopped.

The sun broke through the horizon casting beautiful golden rays of light through the sky. She inhaled, filling her lungs with the briny air.

Dawn brought a new day, a new beginning. This was hers. She needed to grab it with both hands.

Freedom.

Excitement shot all the way to the tips of her toes.

Alejandro needed her. Well, she needed him and *La Rueca*. Jules would do whatever she had to do until the Med Cup was over to create memories that would last a lifetime, ones she could share with her children, and she hoped, someday, with her husband.

Not even thinking about Enrique could burst the enthusiasm energizing her now. Jules wiggled her toes inside her boat shoes. She wanted to be down on the dock. She wanted to sail.

Jules removed the headlamp, switched off the power and shoved the device in her windbreaker's pocket. She hurried down the path, eager to climb aboard *La Rueca*.

Men stood on the dock and in the boat. Navy, black, red and white seemed to be the colors of choice for their clothing. Two wore baseball caps. Good, she wanted to fit in.

Still butterflies filled her stomach. She kept descending moving closer to the boat.

A few men glanced her way, gave her the once-over, but not in the way she was used to. That was okay. She didn't want them looking at her too closely.

She studied each and every one of the faces. The crew contained a mix of nationalities and ages. But she didn't see Alejandro with them.

Anxiety rocketed through her.

Where was he? Alejandro hadn't mentioned not being here on his note. She couldn't do this without him. Jules wanted to stop moving, but that would look odd. She didn't want to make the crew suspicious. She forced one foot in front of the other.

Please be here.

A familiar head with dark hair popped up from below deck. Alejandro.

Relief washed over her. She quickened her pace to reach him—the boat—faster.

With the dark stubble on his face, he looked very much like a pirate captain and king. His smile made her breath catch in her throat. "Good morning, J.V."

The rich, deep sound of his voice made her heart turn over.

Jules acknowledged him with a nod. The less she said, the better. She kept her hands at her sides, too. She didn't want to wave back like a girl, or worse, a princess.

"This is J.V.," Alejandro announced. "The one I told you about. Wait until you see him at the helm. *La Rueca* turns as if she's sailing on rails."

Jules straightened, pleased by his compliment. Living up to his words might be hard. What if she'd gotten lucky the other night with a perfect combination of wind and sea?

The others didn't say anything. They eyed her warily.

Jules wasn't offended. She understood their caution. Alejandro had given her the nod of approval, but she was an unknown quantity. She would have to earn their respect with her sailing. She only hoped she could.

"Hi," Jules said in the deepest voice she could manage.

She shoved her bare hands in her jacket pockets. Shaking hands with anyone would be a bad idea. She'd trimmed her nails and removed the polish, but her hands still looked feminine. Maybe she needed a pair of sailing gloves.

"I'm Phillipe." The bald man with clear, blue eyes spoke with a French accent. She recognized him from races she'd watched on television. "Tactician."

Before she could acknowledge him, Phillipe

walked away, unimpressed by her. Uh-oh. This could be interesting since they would have to work closely together.

"I'm Mike. One of the grinders." The burly, brown-haired man, whose job was to crank the winch, sounded like an American. He yawned. "I hope all our practices aren't going to be at the crack of dawn."

Wanting to say as little as possible, Jules glanced at Alejandro.

"J.V. can't miss any of his classes at the university," he answered. "The wind is good in the morning."

"This morning," Mike agreed. "But these early wake-up calls are going to mess with my social life, skipper."

"Chatting on Facebook can wait until after the Med Cup, mate." A bleach blond with a tanned face stepped forward. Friendliness and warmth emanated from his wide smile. "I work the bow. Sam's the name. From New Zealand. Welcome aboard, J.V."

She smiled at him, feeling a little strange that no one could tell she wasn't a boy. Okay, she didn't want to be recognized, but it made her wonder. Were her features that masculine? Was that the reason her father had such a hard time marrying her off?

"Dude, I'm not talking about Facebook," Mike said to Sam. "This girl I met at the club last night is so hot. She's interested, too."

Sam laughed. "In getting away from you."

"Yeah, right. That's why she gave me her number," Mike countered. "I'm texting her as soon as we finish practice. Talk about an amazing rack."

As a red-haired, Irish-sounding guy asked to see the woman's picture, heat rushed to Jules's cheeks. She turned her face away so no one would notice. Her brothers didn't talk like that in front of her. Not even Brandt, who probably considered admiring "racks" a pastime.

"No pics right now, Cody. We'll finish the rest of the introductions later," Alejandro said. "Let's take advantage of the wind and have J.V. show us what he can do."

Jules swallowed around the anchor-size lump lodged in her throat. If she messed up...

No, she shouldn't imagine making any mistakes.

The other crewmembers took their positions.

Alejandro had put his faith in her. She couldn't let him down.

With her insides shaking, Jules boarded *La Rueca*. She removed Brandt's sunglasses from her pocket and put them on. The dark lenses would protect her eyes from the rising sun, but also hide them.

She was a world away from the life she lived, but her training would help her today. A helmsman needed to be cool, calm, calculating. Just like a princess.

Shoulders back. Chin up. Smile.

Jules did all three. As her fingers tightened around the wheel, she widened her stance. The position felt familiar, comfortable.

"Ready?" Alejandro asked.

She would prove to the crew Alejandro hadn't made a mistake by giving her the helm. "Ready, skipper."

Her smile widened. She sounded like a German. Maybe she could pull this off.

Julianna had done it. Pride filled Alejandro. She'd proved her worth as a helmsman with some world-class sailing.

The three hours on the water went by faster than anyone expected. No one wanted to return to the dock. But Julianna needed to get back to the palace before anyone realized she wasn't asleep in her bed as they thought.

Standing on the dock, Alejandro picked up a line. He glanced at the cockpit where Julianna studied one of Phillipe's charts. With her sunglasses on top of her hat, she looked every bit a teenager. No one suspected differently. Maybe people only saw what they expected to see. The disguise made her appear younger, but nothing could hide her high cheekbones, lush lips or smooth complexion.

Alejandro could watch her all day long and never get bored.

"Skipper," Sam called from the bow. "Toss me the line."

Alejandro did.

"The kid's good." Sam hooked the end around a cleat. "Quiet, but he knows what he's doing. The way he maneuvered around that buoy. Sweet. It's like he's got a sixth sense when it comes to wind shifts."

"Told you."

Sam nodded. "But J.V. seems a bit...soft. We need

to take him out. Harden him up. Make him drink until he pukes."

Alejandro's muscles tensed. Having Julianna out here without a bodyguard was bad enough. Granted, he could protect her. No doubt his security detail wasn't far away given his sneaking out of the palace hadn't been necessary this morning. But he wouldn't put her in harm's way, not even for a little hazing by the crew. "J.V. is young. He lives with his overprotective family. If we have some fun with him like that, he won't be allowed to sail with us."

"Okay, but he's wound pretty tight. Maybe a woman—"

"Leave the kid alone," Alejandro interrupted. "That's an order."

"If you change your mind—"

"The kid's a natural. We need to mentor J.V., not introduce him to a life of debauchery."

"You've never had a problem with debauchery before." Sam grinned knowingly. "Let me guess. The kid has a hot sister."

Julianna was hot. Alejandro smiled.

"You dog." Sam laughed. "I didn't know you liked young pups."

Alejandro didn't. "She's a bit older than J.V., but 'll take what I can get."

That was the case with Julianna until she married. hen he'd be free and she'd be with… He didn't want think about that.

"Okay. I'll put my plans to corrupt the youngster

on hold." Sam winked. "Until you've had your fill of his sister."

A good thing Julianna couldn't hear them. She was huddled with Phillipe going over race strategy in German. No one knew the Frenchman was fluent. Fortunately Julianna was, too. Otherwise her cover would have been blown.

Day one had been a success. Only time would tell what the rest of the days would bring.

But Alejandro was…hopeful.

Jules walked back to the palace through the dark tunnel. The four-footed creatures running alongside her beam of light didn't bother her. Meeting the crew and being accepted by them exhilarated her. The image of Alejandro with his eyes full of pride, a wide smile on his handsome face and the dawning sun gleaming in his hair gave her a boost of energy.

The darkness beyond her headlamp seemed to go on forever, but she didn't care. Jules felt as if she'd already been crowned queen. The only thing she needed was a hot shower. Okay, a nap wouldn't hurt.

She reached the staircase to her closet and climbed the steep, narrow steps to the landing.

Alejandro's plan had worked. Relief flowed through her veins. Sailing on his crew was going to work out fine. She could race and then marry Enrique. No one would know the truth.

Jules pressed on the latch. The secret door opened. She stepped out of the dark passageway and into the closet.

She'd told Yvette not to disturb her this morning and allow her to wake up on her own. But Jules stood at the closet door and listened. No sounds. Yes! Her escape and return had gone off without a hitch.

She closed the secret door.

All she had to do was undress, hide the sailing clothes and—

The closet door opened. Yvette dropped the towel in her hand and gasped.

Stunned, Jules jumped back.

No, no, no, no, no.

Heart pounding, she lurched forward and placed her hand over Yvette's mouth. "Shhhh. Don't scream."

Fear filled Yvette's brown eyes. "Waah wuh wah ma puhsa."

Jules struggled to comprehend the words. She hoped being in the closet would mute their voices. "I'm going to lower my hand. Do not scream. Understand?"

Yvette nodded.

Jules lowered her hand from the maid's mouth. "What did you say?"

"Please don't hurt my princess."

Hurt. Princess. Yvette hadn't recognized her. Jules could still escape.

Her relief lasted no longer than a breath. Escaping into the tunnels wasn't an option. An investigation into the mysterious closet intruder might reveal the tunnels' existence. Worse, she couldn't allow Yvette to be traumatized by this.

Jules's best choice, her only choice, was to come clean and hope for the best. A miracle.

"It's me, Yvette," Jules whispered. "Julianna."

The young woman's brows knotted, but fear remained in her eyes. "Princess Julianna?"

"Yes." Jules pulled off the baseball hat, wig and the nylon cap holding all her hair.

Yvette gasped. "I just saw you asleep in your bed, ma'am."

"You saw pillows and a blond wig," Jules admitted. "Not me."

Yvette stared at her as if she was an extraterrestrial with three eyes, two mouths and purple skin. "What are you doing in your closet dressed like a boy, ma'am?"

The knowledge of the secret tunnels remained safe. For now. "I've been sailing."

Another gasp. "That is forbidden, ma'am."

"Which is the reason for my disguise." Jules needed Yvette to understand what was at stake. "Please, I beg you. Keep my secret in your heart. Never repeat a word of this to anyone."

Especially the tabloids or her father. Fear of discovery made Jules's stomach roll with nausea.

"I don't understand why you would disobey the king, ma'am." The maid sounded dumbfounded. "You've never…"

"I felt as if I had no other choice." In for a penny, in for a pound. Jules needed Yvette's help. That required honesty. Perhaps the truth would bring compassion. "Once I marry Enrique, my life will be the same as it is back home, with similar restrictions. Enrique has forbidden me from sailing again. I know I'm disobeying my father, but I need a taste of freedom. When Alejandro asked me to be on his racing crew—"

"You're sailing with Prince Alejandro?" Yvette's eyes widened, as if scandalized.

Jules nodded.

"But his reputation—"

"May be bad, but I assure you, Prince Alejandro has been a total gentleman."

Unfortunately.

"If King Alaric finds out or Prince Enrique—"

"Neither has to find out. Only Alejandro and you know what I'm doing. The crew thinks I'm a college kid from Germany."

Yvette said nothing. Her eyes looked contemplative. Maybe she was too stunned for words. Or maybe she was totaling how much she could make selling this story to the media.

Jules knew her freedom, at least what little she'd found sailing with Alejandro, would vanish with one wrong word. She took the maid's hands in hers. "I know what I'm asking is wrong, but please don't tell anyone."

The seconds ticked by.

"I'll keep your secret, ma'am," Yvette said. "I pledge my loyalty and promise to help you."

Her words nearly knocked Jules over. "Oh, thank you. I'll find some way to make it up to you. I promise."

"That isn't necessary, ma'am." Compassion shone in Yvette's eyes. "I understand."

"You do?"

"Yes, ma'am. I'd love to escape my job as a palace maid, move to Milan or Paris and work in the fashion industry." Wistfulness echoed in the maid's words.

A kindred spirit. "You have the talent."

"Thank you, ma'am."

"I'm sure we aren't the only ones who wish for something different."

Yvette nodded.

"I can't do much about Paris or Milan, but I can see about getting you a job here on the island."

"Thank you, ma'am, but my family needs me in Aliestle. I don't want to hurt my sisters' marriage prospects."

"I understand, but if you change your mind let me know." Jules had more in common with her maid than she realized. She smiled. "Having your help, Yvette, is going to make sailing in the Med Cup so much easier. Here's what we'll need to do…"

CHAPTER NINE

AS THE DAYS FLEW BY, Jules juggled between playing the role of J.V. and being Princess Julianna. Whenever anyone wanted to see her in the morning, Yvette said the princess was sleeping. No one was the wiser, at the palace or on the crew, in spite of a close call when a strong gust of wind nearly blew her cap and wig off her head.

Jules had found a way to do her duty, as was required by her father and country, and experience freedom, as her heart and soul longed for. But guilt niggled at her.

Being on Alejandro's crew was a crazy, fun adventure, but a temporary one. Her wedding day, however, was right after the Med Cup, yet she'd barely thought about it. Or her groom.

Prince Enrique wasn't the man of her dreams, but he was to be her husband and the father of her children. Their marriage would last for the rest of her life. She couldn't ignore her fiancé, even if he'd been ignoring her.

If love was to blossom, someone had to make

the first move. That someone was going to have to be her.

With her resolve in place, Jules walked to Enrique's office. The sound of her heels against the marble floor echoed through the hall.

Enrique's assistant wasn't behind his desk, but the door to the inner office was ajar.

She tapped lightly. "Enrique?"

"Julianna." He rose from a large walnut desk. His gray suit, white dress shirt and red tie were a far cry from Alejandro's casual boating clothes and sexy, carefree style, but Enrique looked regal and handsome. "What brings you here?"

Jules entered the office. "I've hardly seen you this week."

She preferred sailing with Alejandro or her own company to being with Enrique. But she needed to make sure their marriage started out on a solid footing even if he saw her as nothing more than his royal broodmare and arm candy.

"True, but I've been thinking about you." Enrique smiled, but the gesture seemed to be more of an effort to placate her. "You must understand, my princess. There is much work to attend to."

"Yes, you have been busy." She wanted him to show her she hadn't misjudged him. She wanted him to do something to make her want to be with him the way she wanted to be with Alejandro. "Will you be joining us for dinner tonight?"

Enrique hadn't eaten with them the past four nights. Not even her father worked that much, and he was king. Aliestle was a small country, but wealthier and more influential than this island.

"I regret missing dinners." Enrique motioned to the papers on his desk. "But I am working more now so I can take a few days off after the wedding."

I, not we. Disappointment weighed her down. For their marriage to work, she needed Enrique to meet her halfway. "Just a few days for our honeymoon?"

He nodded. "I can't afford to be away any longer."

"I understand." Look at the bright side, Jules thought. They hadn't spent any time alone. Whenever they attended an official event, a security detail and the press accompanied them. And each time they were together, Enrique managed to irritate her more. A short honeymoon might be best. "Duty first."

He sat. "Your sense of duty appeals to me, Julianna."

Her obedience was second only to her dowry.

Stay positive. Enrique might want to lead her around like a champion show dog on a leash, but their daughters could be doctors and lawyers if they were raised on La Isla de la Aurora. Jules forced a smile. "Thank you."

"How is the wedding planning coming along?" he asked.

The question struck her as odd. Enrique made most of the decisions about the royal wedding. Either he was trying to be polite or he thought her that clueless. Neither boded well. But she kept her pride in check.

"The wedding coordinators seem to have everything in hand. But I manage to keep myself...occupied."

Her day started at 3:00 a.m. in preparation for the morning sails. Jules returned to the palace for more sleep before heading to town to make appearances and attend functions.

"I love going into the capital," she admitted.

The coastal town looked like something from a postcard with its pastel buildings with tiled roofs, the coffee shops with umbrella covered tables and the open-air markets where people could buy everything from fresh fish to vegetables. Businesses closed in the afternoon for siesta. The relaxed pace reminded her of Alejandro.

Don't think about him now.

"The people are charming," she added.

The citizens of La Isla de la Aurora embraced their Spanish heritage. They spoke English and Spanish with ease often mixing the two languages. Wherever she went, smiles greeted her. The genuine warmth of the people touched her heart. Jules felt accepted here in a way she'd never felt back home. That gave her another reason for wanting this marriage to work. She liked living on the island.

"You've been tired lately," he said with what sounded like a hint of concern. She was surprised he'd noticed.

"A little." Jules made do with what sleep she could squeeze in. "I'm working hard to learn my new role."

Here at the palace and on the boat.

"You're doing well." He sounded pleased. "I saw your picture in the paper this morning. You were at the hospital."

She nodded. "I enjoy visiting the patients, especially the children. There's this little boy. His name is—"

"Stop visiting the hospital until after the wedding," he interrupted. "You could catch a nasty germ there."

"I'm sure you wouldn't want to get sick." The words slipped out.

"That's for certain."

She swallowed a sigh. Once again he was only concerned about himself. "I'm just tired, Enrique. Don't be concerned about catching germs, I'm healthy."

"I know."

Jules drew back. "You do?"

"Our palace doctor spoke with yours."

She didn't know what to say. Had all her fiancés been told about her medical record? Not that she had anything to hide, but still… She hated the lack of privacy. That would never happen to one of her brothers.

Enrique glanced at his computer monitor, distracted by whatever had popped up on his screen. "Is there anything else?"

No, you egotistical tyrant-wannabe, Jules would have said if she had a choice, but she didn't say a word. Like it or not, Enrique was going to be her husband. She couldn't spend the rest of her life fantasizing about his younger brother. She had to make this relationship with Enrique work. Somehow.

"Perhaps we could go out," she suggested. "Just the two of us. On a date," she clarified, so he got the point.

"A date. What a sweet thought. But that's not possible with our upcoming nuptials." He placed his fingers on his keyboard. "Don't fret, my princess. We'll have plenty of time for dates after we're married."

Their first kiss would be at the wedding ceremony. Their first date would be on their honeymoon. The thought of her wedding night made her nauseous.

She straightened. "I'll leave you to your work."

Enrique didn't look up. He didn't mutter a goodbye. The only sound was his fingers tapping on the keyboard.

So much for meeting her halfway. She walked to the doorway.

Time to face facts. If not for the PR opportunity at the wedding, he'd send a proxy to stand in for him as groom at the ceremony.

Enrique was going to have to have a complete change of heart about her and the marriage for things to work. Even then she wondered if love was possible.

But Jules knew one thing. No longer would she feel any guilt for sailing. She'd tried to make things better, but Enrique had shut her down.

Nothing was going to stop her from having the time of her life with Alejandro and the crew. Nothing at all.

* * *

Alejandro couldn't focus. All he wanted to do was look at the picture of Julianna on the cover of this morning's newspaper. He stared at the black and white photograph.

No one would call this vibrant, warm woman an ice princess. The smile on her face reached all the way to her eyes. Those same eyes looked brighter, more alive.

Alejandro wondered if he—make that the sailing— had brought about those changes. Or had it been Enrique?

He hadn't seen the royal couple together in a few days. Enrique had skipped several dinners. Alejandro hadn't minded one bit. He enjoyed spending time and talking with Julianna even with his father and Brandt there. The more Alejandro learned about her, the more he wanted to know. He couldn't wait to see her tonight.

He glanced at the clock. Only two.

The thought of waiting until dinnertime to see Julianna didn't sit well. If he returned to the palace early, he could see if she wanted to spend time with Boots. She enjoyed playing with the kitten.

Alejandro liked playing with her. Or would, if he could...

He'd settle for being alone with her.

She might be on his boat every morning, but so was the rest of the crew. They couldn't talk openly or in a language he was comfortable speaking. She had to play a role, and so did he.

Leaving with her from the dock might raise

suspicions, so she always headed back to the palace alone while he went off to the boatyard.

He looked at the clock again.

Why not take the afternoon off? He rarely did so.

After a quick talk with the boatyard foreman about what needed to be completed today, Alejandro returned to the palace. He found Boots sound asleep in the apartment. The kitten didn't stir when Alejandro picked him up. He went to Julianna's room and knocked on her door.

No answer.

Alejandro knocked again. Nothing.

Damn. He felt becalmed, as if all the wind had left his sails.

"Are you looking for Princess Julianna, sir?"

He turned to face one of the palace housekeepers with a feather duster in her hand. "Yes, Elena, I brought Boots by for a visit."

"Every day the princess tells me how much the kitten is growing." Elena's smile deepened the lines on her face. She'd been working at the palace for as long as he could remember. She used to sneak him food when he'd been grounded for some infraction or other. "The princess is right, sir."

Alejandro hadn't noticed any changes in the kitten. He glanced down. Boots may have gained some weight. But they'd only been living at the palace a little over a week. That didn't seem long enough for the kitten to grow.

Then again Alejandro felt as if he'd known Julianna for years not days. He felt so comfortable around her. "The princess has been sneaking Boots treats. That's probably why."

Elena nodded. "I saw the princess head down to the beach about a half an hour ago."

"Thank you."

Alejandro returned the kitten to the apartment and then headed to the beach.

Clear blue waves rolled to shore. Off in the distance, Julianna sat on the sand. She didn't seem concerned about her white Capri pants getting dirty.

A seabird soared overhead. The white wings contrasted against the blue sky. Another bird swooped and dipped its feet into the water, but the talons came up empty.

Julianna wasn't alone. Her bodyguard, Klaus, stood back. Far enough to give the princess privacy but close enough to react if needed. Alejandro acknowledged Klaus with a nod before approaching Julianna.

As he made his way toward Julianna, the wind caught in her hair. Strands went every which way. She pushed the hair off her face.

He would have liked to do that for her. He remembered how her hair felt, soft as silk, when strands had slipped out of her wig. But with Klaus behind them, Alejandro would have to keep his hands to himself. "Hello, Princess."

Julianna glanced up at him. The combination of

the sky and her short-sleeved shirt accentuated the blueness of her eyes. She smiled, looking pleased to see him. "Hi."

"Enjoying the peace and quiet?"

"Yes. I was raised to fear being on my own, but I like it." She raised a handful of sand into the air and let the granules sift from her fingers. A hill of sand formed. "Especially out here by the water."

"I don't want to disturb you."

"You're not." She patted the spot next to her. "Sit."

He did.

Julianna carved into the sand until a rustic castle took shape.

"You need a bucket and a shovel to build a proper castle," he said.

She stuck out her tongue. "Who said anything about this being proper?"

He laughed. "My mistake."

"This castle is different. Special."

Her wistful tone intrigued him. "Tell me about it."

"In this castle, you're allowed to do whatever you choose. The only rule is to follow your heart."

Alejandro shoved his hands into the warm sand to help her dig a moat. "A good rule for any castle, proper or not."

She nodded. "Marriage is encouraged, but only if you've found your one true love."

His hands worked right next to hers. If he moved his left hand, he could touch her. The bodyguard would be none the wiser. Klaus couldn't see past their backs or hear what they were saying. Alejandro inched his hand closer. "Weddings must be rare."

One side of the castle collapsed. She knocked the rest away and started over. "Divorces are rarer."

A little farther… Anticipation built.

Alejandro wanted to touch her, to feel her soft skin against his once more, but doing so would be wrong. He moved his hand away from hers.

"That would be a different kind of castle." While she occupied herself making another mound of sand, Alejandro pulled out his phone, typed in a text message for Ortiz and hit Send. "What about royal duty?"

"Royalty does not exist."

That surprised him. Sailing aside, she seemed so keen on being a perfect princess and having little princes and princesses to keep the royal bloodline going.

"All people are created equal in my castle," she continued. "Whether male or female, wealthy or poor."

"Sounds like a nice place to live."

"It would be nice." Jules stared at the sand. "If I could build it."

The longing in her voice touched his heart. "La Isla de la Aurora isn't perfect, but it's an enjoyable place to live. Though you won't have the kind of freedom here as you'd have in your castle."

She laughed. "It's a fantasy. No place like that exists."

"True." But the freedom he craved did. Her marriage to Enrique would give Alejandro what he wanted. No more pressure or orders to fulfill his royal duties and obligations. Yet was marriage to his brother what Julianna wanted?

"Your castle may be a fantasy, but if that's your dream I don't understand why you want to marry Enrique."

"It's my duty."

"You have a duty to yourself."

She stopped digging in the sand. "I was raised to do whatever is best for Aliestle. I've always known a marriage would be arranged for me. That is the custom. And marrying Enrique is what's best for my family and my country."

She sounded genuine. Patriotic. Alejandro's respect for her grew knowing the sacrifice she was making. "You hold duty in a much higher esteem than I do. You're ready to dive headfirst into an arranged marriage knowing you're sacrificing your dreams. I can't wait to escape the demands of palace life. We are very different."

Her gaze met his. "You want what's best for your country."

"Yes."

"So do I. We're just going about it differently."

Julianna might think so, but he knew better. She was far more worthy than him. "My brother doesn't deserve you."

She shrugged. "He would say I don't deserve

him the way I've been sneaking around behind his back."

Alejandro sprung to her defense. "You're helping the island. Once we place—"

"Win."

Her confidence pleased him. "Yes, win, I'll be able to draw more attention to the sailing and tourism here. But my father and brother..."

"They have different ideas."

"They have taken a completely different path," Alejandro said. "Enrique thinks my efforts are too radical. He believes a royal wedding will accomplish the same thing as my plans." Alejandro drew lines in the sand. He wanted to make his own mark somehow. "But I'm not going to let them stop me. I'll turn this economy around and show them."

"I'm certain you will."

He appreciated her confidence. He also liked how her blond hair shone beneath the afternoon sun. So beautiful.

One of the garden staff sprinted across the beach with his arms loaded with colorful buckets, shovels and other sand tools. He placed them on the sand. "Compliments of Ortiz, Your Highnesses."

Julianna's grin lit up her face. "Please thank him for me."

The young man bowed before walking away.

She shot Alejandro a suspicious glance. "You sent a text to Ortiz asking for all this."

"Sometimes being a prince comes in handy."

The gratitude sparkling in her eyes made it difficult for Alejandro to breathe. "Thank you."

He ignored the quickening of his pulse and handed her one of the shovels. "Let's see if we can build you a castle that will last."

CHAPTER TEN

THAT EVENING, Jules floated down the staircase on her way to dinner. Her sling-back heels felt more like ballet slippers as she descended and the hem of her cocktail dress swooshed above her knees. An afternoon with Alejandro had been exactly what she needed. Building a sand castle had been fun, but being with him had made her heart sing. He'd told her about growing up on the island and listened when she spoke. Something men in Aliestle, including her brothers, rarely did.

Jules wondered if he was in the dining room. Anticipation danced through her. She couldn't talk to him as freely as she had on the beach, but being with him during the meal would be enough.

Realization dawned. She had a huge crush on him.

She giggled like a schoolgirl. That would explain her growing affection toward him. Though crushing on her future brother-in-law probably broke every rule in the princess handbook.

Well, she never claimed to be perfect. Besides, she'd never let the crush go anywhere.

She entered the dining room to find Alejandro and Enrique involved in a heated discussion. As soon as they saw her they stopped talking.

She saw three place settings on the table large enough to seat twenty-four. "Is no one else joining us?"

Enrique kissed the top of her hand. He seemed big on that gesture. But he'd made an effort. She shouldn't complain.

"My father is dining with old friends," he said.

"Brandt is dining with new friends," Alejandro explained. "He took Klaus with him."

No doubt with a push from Alejandro. She would have to thank him later. "Lucky me. I'm a fortunate woman to be dining with two handsome princes."

Enrique stared down his nose at his brother. "Though one of us is handsomer than the other."

Alejandro half-laughed. "In your dreams, bro."

Jules wondered what Enrique would do or say. She hoped nothing.

He ignored his brother and escorted her to the table. That pleased Jules. But his stiff formality overshadowed how suave and debonair he looked tonight in his dark suit. If only he would relax and not always be so...on.

A footman pulled out her chair, and she sat. A server placed a napkin across her lap.

Alejandro took his seat in one easy, fluid motion. He was definitely relaxed. Still he looked stylish in his own right wearing a button-down shirt and black pants. Not too fancy, but not casual. Just...right.

Her admiring gaze met his and lingered. The temperature in the room seemed to increase. Her heart rate kicked up a notch.

His mouth quirked.

Oh, no. He must realize she was staring.

Jules looked away. She took a sip of ice water, but the liquid did nothing to cool her down.

Enrique sat at the head of the table in King Dario's place. The ornate chair befit the king with his confidence and majestic splendor better than his son, who didn't quite emanate the right amount of regality and power. In time that would come, Jules told herself. With more…maturity.

The light from the chandeliers dimmed. Lit candles in foot- tall crystal holders provided a warm glow. Platinum-rimmed china set atop silver chargers stood out on the crisp, white linen tablecloth. A stunning bouquet of roses and lilies in an elaborate silver vase added a light floral fragrance to the air.

A table fit for a future king. And queen, she reminded herself.

"Romantic," Alejandro said.

Very. She forced her gaze off him and onto Enrique. This would be the perfect opportunity for her fiancé to show Jules he was willing to make an effort with their relationship. Oh, she wanted to dine with Alejandro, but if Enrique held out an olive branch, or a red rose in this case, she would gladly accept what he offered.

"You know." Alejandro pushed back from the table.

"I'm sure you both would prefer an intimate dinner for two."

He glanced at Jules. She didn't know whether to thank him for the suggestion or not. Her heart debated with her mind over the outcome each wanted. She looked at Enrique, holding her breath while waiting for his answer.

"That's generous of you, but the table is set for three. You're already seated," Enrique said. "Please stay and dine with us. I'd like to finish our discussion."

Relief mingled with disappointment. Jules would get to spend more time with Alejandro, but Enrique should have taken his brother up on his offer. If he'd listened to her in his office, he would have jumped at the opportunity for them to share a romantic dinner alone.

But he hadn't, and he didn't.

Was he that dense or was he trying to make some kind of point? Did he want a chaperone present so rumors couldn't start? No matter what the reason, his decision stung.

She stared into her water glass, not wanting to participate in the brothers' conversation about Alejandro's most recent real estate purchase—a run-down hotel on the opposite side of the island.

The servers brought out the first course. Gazpacho.

Jules waited for Enrique to take the first sip, then did so herself. The cold tomato-based soup was one of her favorites. This version had a little more spices than she was used to, but she liked the tanginess.

Enrique wiped his mouth with a napkin. "I heard

the two of you were out on the beach building sand castles today."

Jules stirred uneasily. She didn't want to risk saying too much so took a sip of white wine. The Albarino tasted crisp and fresh, a perfect complement to the acidity in the soup.

"Yes, I bumped into Julianna on the beach," Alejandro said much to her relief. "She was having trouble making a sand castle with her hands so I asked Ortiz to send out some proper tools to use."

"Tools." Enrique snickered. "You mean, toys."

Alejandro didn't look at his brother. He picked up his wineglass and sipped, the same way she had.

Jules recognized the impatience in his eyes. He was trying hard not to say anything. She respected him for not losing his temper. It couldn't be easy letting so much roll off his back. Maybe she could make it a little easier on him this time. He'd come to her assistance by speaking up before, now she could return the favor.

"Having the buckets and tools delivered was a sweet gesture." The afternoon had been a pure delight. The time had flown by with all the talking and laughter. She'd shared her dreams with Alejandro, something she'd never done with anyone else. Not even Brandt.

But Alejandro made her feel safe and, like the people on this island, accepted. He seemed to know her so well—better than her own family. It was easy to open up around him. He'd become a good…friend.

"And much appreciated," she added for Alejandro's

benefit. "I would have never been able to build my castle without those items. Especially one that…"

"Lasts." Alejandro raised his glass to her. "Now everyone can live…"

"Happily ever after," she said with a smile.

"You shouldn't have been out there so long." Enrique scowled, seemingly oblivious to how close she'd gotten to his brother. "You're sunburned."

Jules touched her face. "Where?"

He studied her as if she were flawed and should be returned to the store for a refund. "Your nose."

"Fair skin," she said.

"I didn't notice it when you were in my office," Enrique said.

Thank goodness this hadn't been the result of sailing. That would have been a total disaster. "I must not have put on enough sunscreen this afternoon."

"The sun is strong here," Alejandro said. "I should have reminded you."

Enrique nodded, one of the few times she'd seen him agree with his brother. "Makeup will hide the redness. But if you get sunburned any worse, the wedding pictures will be ruined."

Jules knew he expected her to make him look good. She'd have to layer zinc oxide on her nose during the race. Not only would that protect her skin from the sun's harsh rays, but the thick, white lotion would help disguise her face better. "I'll be more careful when we're out tomorrow."

Enrique eyed her suspiciously. "Planning to build more sand castles?

A lot more careful. She swallowed. Another sunburn would be a dead giveaway she wasn't spending much of the daylight hours asleep in her bed. "No, but I plan to be outside. I was hoping you could join me."

Alejandro nodded his approval.

Enrique didn't notice. "I have meetings."

"You've heard about our afternoon, Enrique," Alejandro said. "Tell us about yours."

"It was more interesting than playing in the sand." Enrique described his day in minute detail.

Jules mouthed the word "thanks." She appreciated Alejandro shifting the focus off her and onto Enrique's favorite subject—himself.

Courses paired with wines to complement the flavors of the dish came and went. Enrique droned on with Alejandro chiming in with comments spoken and muttered under this breath.

The differences between the two brothers became more distinct. Enrique was so focused on himself and his role as crown prince and future king, nothing else mattered. She wasn't sure if he cared who sat at the table with him as long as someone was present to hear him speak.

But Alejandro wasn't perfect, either. His blatant disdain for the responsibilities thrust upon him by his royal birth and his lack of respect for the monarchy made her question his priorities. She wished he wasn't so intent on turning his back on his duty.

Still she enjoyed his company. No one had ever made her feel so...good, capable, alive. Underneath his casual, sailor exterior, Jules saw a man—a prince—who loved his country with his whole heart, the same as her. But he'd been pushed aside due to the birth order and forced to live in Enrique's shadow. And for that, he blamed the monarchy and the rules that accompanied it.

Neither brother was Prince Charming, and that was okay. Such a prince was the thing of legends and fairy tales, like the expectation of her being the perfect princess. Being perfect wasn't possible.

Too bad no one else seemed to realize that.

Jules slumped in her chair, overcome by weariness and emotion. She straightened only to want to relax again. She focused on the food and tried to tune everything else out. It wasn't hard to do.

As soon as the servers cleared the dessert dishes, Jules wiped her mouth and folded her napkin. "Thank you for the pleasant company, gentlemen. I'm going to retire for the evening."

Both men rose as she stood.

"Good night, Julianna," Alejandro said.

"Sleep well," Enrique said. "I want to see my bride's pretty blue eyes sparkling tomorrow."

She moved away from her chair and waited for Enrique to offer to escort her, but his feet remained rooted in place.

Alejandro's gaze met hers in silent understanding. "Sweet dreams."

Jules acknowledged him with a smile. She didn't dare trust her voice. She wanted to have sweet dreams.

but she feared the wrong brother would be starring in them. Not only tonight.

But every night for the rest of her life.

Alejandro's temper flared, but he maintained control.

For Julianna's sake.

She walked out of the dining room with her head high, but the disappointment in her eyes was unmistakable.

Alejandro remained standing until she disappeared from sight. He turned to Enrique. "Why didn't you escort Julianna to her room?"

Enrique had already sat. He motioned to the wine steward to refill his empty glass. "She said she was tired."

Anger burned in Alejandro's throat. "That's why you should have walked with her."

His brother's gaze sharpened. "Why do you care what I do with Julianna?"

Good question. Alejandro sat. He downed what remained in his wineglass. He wanted to say he felt indifferent about her, but he would be lying. He enjoyed being with her whether on the boat or here at the palace. But, rudeness aside, that didn't explain why his brother's treatment of her bothered him so much. "I wouldn't want her to leave the island."

That much was true.

"Never fear, little brother." Enrique snickered. "She can't leave."

"Can't?"

"If Julianna doesn't marry me, she'll be forced to marry a nobleman from Aliestle." His lip curled in disgust. "Any woman with half a brain would want out of that backward country."

Alejandro hated that she had only those two options. She deserved so much more. "Julianna has more than half a brain. She's very intelligent."

"That is why she doesn't mind how I treat her. She knows she must marry me," Enrique explained. "She'll put up with anything I do or say to keep from having to spend the rest of her life stuck in archaic Aliestle where men treat her worse."

Julianna had admitted as much to Alejandro, but that didn't excuse Enrique's behavior. "Her misfortunate situation gives you carte blanche to be ill-mannered and rude to her. How...noble."

Enrique snorted. "This is rich. Relationship advice from the man who goes through women as if they were selections on a menu."

"I may have never been involved in a serious relationship for an extended period of time, but I know women. Better, it seems, than you, bro," Alejandro said. "Julianna isn't an obedient automaton. She has feelings. Dreams. She deserves—"

"She deserves what I see fit to give her."

"Enrique..."

"As long as she obeys and provides me with heirs be assured she'll have all she needs."

"She needs to be loved and accepted for who she is," Alejandro countered. "If you continue treating her poorly and taking advantage of her situation, you'll alienate her until she can't take it anymore. Is that what you want?"

Enrique leaned back in their father's chair. "You've come up with all this about her after spending an afternoon playing in the sand?"

"You've missed dinners this week," Alejandro replied. "You can learn a lot about a person over seven course meals."

Especially Julianna once she let her guard down and opened up.

"Come on, Alejandro," Enrique cajoled. "You don't care about Julianna. You want to make sure I marry."

"With your marriage comes my freedom from royal obligations."

That was the one thing Alejandro wanted more than anything. Somehow with his growing concerns over Julianna's future he'd lost sight of that. How had that happened?

Letting physical attraction and friendship get in the way of what he wanted made no sense. Julianna was hot, but she was also a princess. She might enjoy sailing, but she would never walk away from her title or her duty. Not for anything in the world. She wanted to help her brother, her country and her future children. The fact that she was willing to marry Enrique after his treatment of her spoke volumes about her priorities and was a not-so-subtle reminder…

As soon as the Med Cup finished and she married, Alejandro needed to say goodbye. She belonged with his brother, not him.

The truth stung. A sharp pain sliced into his heart. He reached for his wineglass, but it was empty.

"Treat her better." If Enrique did that, he would give Julianna what she wanted—more freedom, a throne and children.

Especially children.

I've always wanted to be a mother. Children will bring me great happiness and joy. I'll devote myself to being the best mother I can be. That will make me very happy.

Julianna's words echoed inside Alejandro's head. He wanted her to be happy. That wasn't like him. He'd never considered a woman's happiness beyond the moment at hand. He hadn't worried about how she felt after. That didn't make him much better than Enrique who wasn't considering Julianna's happiness at all.

The truth hit Alejandro like a sucker punch.

He didn't want to have anything in common with his brother.

"Do it for yourself, but for me and the island, too." And Julianna. "Heirs must be your first priority."

Enrique's forehead creased. "You want out of the line of succession that badly?"

"Yes." Alejandro did. But this wasn't about him anymore. Julianna needed babies to love. He was finally figuring out why this had become important to him.

Maybe if she were happy, he might be happy, too.

* * *

Alejandro tossed and turned all night. Images of Julianna flashed in his mind like photographs in a digital picture frame. Her long legs exposed by her short dress. Her playful smile on the beach. Her parted lips as she steered *La Rueca*. Her passion-filled eyes as she looked at him.

The last one was pure fantasy.

With a grimace, Alejandro tried to fall asleep for the fourth time. But he couldn't stop the slide show playing in his brain. He kept thinking about her, about wanting to be with her, about wanting to touch her.

Not only touch her.

Alejandro punched his pillow. Maybe if he was more comfortable…

Nothing helped. The harder he tried not to think about her, the more he did. Some of the thoughts were going to require a cold shower if he wasn't careful.

He didn't want to take that chance. He jumped out of bed, dressed for sailing and headed to the boat.

That would keep him…distracted.

La Rueca bobbed in the water. This past week, he'd gotten used to the activity of the crew preparing for a sail or cleaning up afterward. Today, she looked lonely tied to the dock with her running lights off and no crew around.

Better remedy that. Alejandro hopped aboard. The boat rocked with the incoming tides. The wind increased, jostling the lines that secured the boat to the dock. Metal clanked against metal. The waves picked up momentum, hitting the hull with more force.

He glanced at the horizon. Orange and red fingers of sunlight poked their way into the dark sky.

Red sky at night, sailor's delight. Red sky at morning, sailor's warning.

The nursery rhyme used to predict weather played in his head. A red sky might mean a more challenging sail this morning. That would be a good test for the crew with the race coming up.

Especially Julianna.

He had no doubt she'd rise to the challenge. The more situations she was exposed to, the more experience she could rely upon come race day. He'd have to make sure they came up with a good excuse to explain her absence during the three days of races. Sleeping in late wouldn't cut it.

An image of Julianna's twinkling blue eyes, her smiling mouth and her sunburned nose formed in his mind. At least that picture was more innocent than others he'd imagined.

He laughed.

"Care to let me in on the joke?"

Alejandro's heart lurched. He could recognize Julianna's melodic voice anywhere.

He whipped around to face the dock. The beam of light from her headlamp blinded him. He shielded his eyes. "You're here early."

She removed her headlamp, turned it off and shoved it in her pocket. "Couldn't sleep."

Her, too. Alejandro doubted for the same reason as him.

Lust probably wasn't in the innocent princess's

ocabulary. Not that anyone would mistake Julianna
or anything but a too thin, gawky teen in those baggy
lothes.

Anyone, except him.

He saw a beautiful woman who was willing to dis-
uise herself to experience a taste of freedom. She'd
rabbed the golden ring with both hands and wasn't
oing to let go until she had to. Julianna was…special.
He'd never met a woman like her. If only…

Don't go there. He'd decided what he needed to do
nce she married. But she was here now.

Alejandro shifted his weight. He needed some dis-
ance. "I'm going to get the sails."

He stepped below deck without waiting for her to
espond. He didn't want to care what she said.

A musty scent filled his nostrils. He'd always found
amiliarity in the smell, but he would have rather
reathed in Julianna's sweet fragrance. Her usual
cent when she wasn't pretending to be a teenage
oy.

He shook his head. She'd gotten under his skin. He
eeded to get her out of there.

Alejandro felt a presence behind him. He didn't need
o turn around to know who it was. "Julianna."

"I'll help you."

"Thanks." He faced her. The sails, equipment and
ope of the hull didn't leave a lot of room. With her
own here, the space felt more cramped. Or maybe
e was more aware of her. "But I've got them."

"We'll have things ready for the crew faster with
wo pairs of hands."

He'd said something similar to her after their first sail together. That seemed like a lifetime ago.

The boat tilted to one side, as if hit by a mischievous wind or a powerful surge.

Julianna widened her stance.

The boat jolted and leaned the opposite way. Jules flew into Alejandro. He caught her, as he had in the foyer that first morning when she'd arrived at the palace.

He stared down at her face. Her body pressed against his. "The princess is in my arms yet again."

She was nothing like the woman he'd held then. Or maybe she'd taken off the mask and allowed her true self to show. Whichever, he didn't want to let her go. His arms tightened around her.

Attraction sizzled. A need burned deep within him. He fought against the ache with every ounce of self control he had.

The race began tomorrow. The royal wedding would occur next week. She would be out of his life...

The same longing he felt filled Julianna's eyes. Her lips parted.

A sense of urgency drove him. He lowered his mouth to hers, capturing her lips with a kiss.

She gasped, but didn't back away.

His lips ran over hers, tasting and soaking up her sweetness. He knew he was crossing the line.

What he was doing was wrong on so many levels.

But he didn't care. Maybe he'd care later, but at this moment the kiss consumed him. She consumed him.

Julianna arched toward him, her breasts pressing against his chest, her arms entwining around his chest. She opened her mouth further, deepening the kiss. Her eagerness thrilled him. Blood roared through his veins. He pulled her closer, until he felt the rapid beat of her heart.

His tongue explored her mouth with abandon, burning with her sweet heat. Sensation pulsated wildly through him. Passion grew. Self-control slipped.

A soft moan escaped her throat. So sexy.

Alejandro wanted more. He wanted all of her. But he'd take whatever she was willing to give him.

He leaned back against the sail bags, pulling her with him. His hands cupped her round bottom. Fabric bunched. Too much clothing was in the way.

Alejandro slid his hand under her jacket and…

Voices sounded above them.

Julianna jerked away so fast she almost fell on her butt. She regained her balance and touched her hand to her mouth. "I-I'm sorry. I shouldn't have…"

Her red cheeks and ragged breathing made her look so turned-on and sexy, but Alejandro couldn't pretend he didn't hear the regret in her voice. He tried to regain control. Not easy with his body on fire and aching for more kisses. More Julianna.

But she was right. They shouldn't have done this.

"I'm the one who kissed you." He knew better, but

when he was around her he couldn't think straight. "I apologize."

She stared down her nose at him. "I kissed you back."

Always the princess even when passion filled her eyes, a flush stained her neck and cheeks and her lips were swollen. Alejandro bit back a smile. She would be upset if he thought this was funny.

"Alejandro?" Phillipe yelled.

"Ju—J.V. is helping me with the sails." Alejandro needed to calm down and cool off. Or they would blow her cover. But he couldn't stop thinking how perfect her lips felt against his. He'd kissed many women, but no kiss had ever felt like this. "Be up in a minute," he added, not wanting anyone to come down here.

"What now?" she asked.

More kisses. That was what he wanted. But Julianna wasn't some woman he'd met at a club or on the beach or at a sailing regatta. She was Enrique's future wife and Alejandro's ticket out of the royal life he abhorred. Even if his brother was out of the picture, she wasn't a fling. He wasn't looking to get serious with anyone.

Alejandro had too much going on with his boat business, properties and plans for the island to get involved in a serious relationship with any woman. Let alone with a princess.

He wanted to be freed from his princely duties, not be caught up trying to live up to her expectations. She would want him to remain a prince. She would challenge him to be more and embrace his birthright. He'd seen her act that way with Brandt. That behavior and pressure didn't appeal to Alejandro in the slightest. He'd spent too much of his life justifying himself and his actions. Continuing on that path would be hell on earth.

Julianna was the last woman Alejandro should want to be with. She was a perfect princess, with a royal heart and soul. Duty and country motivated her. She would use her role on La Isla de la Aurora to make a difference in Aliestle. He would never be able to make a princess like her happy. He wouldn't want to try. Even if he liked kissing her.

And wanted to kiss her again.

So what now?

"We sail," he answered.

CHAPTER ELEVEN

THREE HOURS OF sailing with high winds and waves kept Jules's mind off Alejandro's kisses. Thank goodness she'd needed to focus on steering the boat, or she would have been sighing, staring and swooning.

Pathetic.

But she couldn't help herself. The way Alejandro made her feel overwhelmed Jules. Which was why she'd hurried up the dock back toward safety without a word as soon as the crew was ready to leave.

She may have apologized, but it wasn't because kissing Alejandro had felt wrong. Kissing him had felt oh-so-right. As if that was what she should be doing today, tomorrow and every day for the rest of her life. That was why she'd been sorry. Feeling that way while engaged to Enrique wasn't fair to either man.

She jogged through the park, eager to return to the palace and the sanctuary of her room. The suite provided all she needed—a means to escape and a lovely view from the windows. Enrique had been right about that. The pretty, colorful blossoms soothed her. She could use some soothing now.

Enrique.

She wove her way through the rocks in the grotto, passed through the wrought-iron gate and locked it behind her.

She didn't want to think about her fiancé now.

Not with the effects of Alejandro's kisses lingering.

The tunnel seemed darker and longer, and the smell of moisture and mold more pronounced. Each of her nerve endings seemed heightened in sensitivity. Her lips still tingled. The ache deep inside her that had started the moment his lips captured hers had grown exponentially since then.

Alejandro stirred something inside her. She was torn by her desire of wanting more and her guilt of knowing better.

Was this what passion felt like?

If so, the feeling frightened her even as it thrilled her. Allowing herself to be carried away by the strong current of emotion would be stupid. She had to be rational about this.

He hadn't proclaimed his undying love and affection. He'd simply kissed her until she couldn't think straight. He'd made her feel so special, like the only woman in the world.

Would that be the only time she ever felt like that? Her heart hoped not.

"Julianna."

The sound of Alejandro's voice sent a shiver of pleasure down her spine, but brought a twinge of uncertainty, too. She stopped walking. "I thought you were going to the boatyard."

He caught up to her. The beam from his flashlight pointed at the dirt floor. "I wanted…"

You. She held her breath.

"…to talk with you," he finished.

Disappointment squeezed her heart even though she knew his wanting her was as likely as her living happily ever after.

Alejandro reached forward and tilted her headlamp so the light shone up. "We never got a chance to talk on the boat."

Her uncertainty increased three-fold. "A hard day of sailing. We needed to focus."

"You didn't smile much."

"I had a lot on my mind." Like now. She started walking. "I should get back to the palace."

Being so close to him sent her out-of-whack emotions spiraling into the danger zone. His scent made her want to lean in closer for another sniff. His warmth made her want to seek shelter in his arms. And his lips made her want to forget what her future held.

He fell into step next to her, his flashlight swinging at his side. "Tell me what's on your mind."

"You mean on the boat?"

"And now."

Jules didn't know where to start. She took a deep breath. It didn't help.

"Julianna," he prompted.

"You. You were…are…on my mind." There, she'd

said it. Even though she figured Alejandro had guessed as much.

"You've been on my mind, too. We're equal."

Not even close. Jules had never felt this way about any man, not even Christian, whom she believed at the time she loved. Of course, she'd been sixteen then.

Not that she was in love with Alejandro. Except...

She wanted to be with him on the boat, off the boat, all the time. She wanted to sneak out of the palace for good and sail off into the sunset with him. And Boots. They wouldn't have to sail—they could walk, run, drive or fly. She wasn't particular on the mode of transportation as long as they were together. The thought of being without Alejandro...

What was she thinking?

Being with him was impossible. What she felt now was a crush. The new sensations he had awakened with his kiss were causing her to feel this way.

Not...love.

"About this morning below deck," Alejandro said.

"It's okay." Jules didn't dare look at him. No one could ever know how much his kisses had affected her. "Each time I exit this tunnel, I enter a whole new world full of wonderful, but forbidden things. Freedom. Sailing. Kissing."

"You've never—"

"I've been kissed." The surprise in his voice made her cheeks grow hot. Jules was embarrassed enough by letting a crush get so out of control. She wasn't about to tell him she could count on one hand the number of times she'd been kissed. "But I'm not... as experienced as you."

"I couldn't tell."

Well, she *could* tell *he* was an expert kisser. That kind of expertise took...practice.

Alejandro has a horrible reputation. Worse, his taste in women is far from discriminating. Royalty, commoner, palace staff, it doesn't matter.

Yvette's words were the cold dose of reality Jules needed. She was probably one in a long line of women who'd come before. A part of her—okay, her heart— didn't want to believe that, but she'd allowed this to go way further than it should. Romanticizing his kisses made no sense. "Kissing you was a nice addition to my adventure."

"Adventure?"

She nodded. "Escaping the palace, wearing a disguise and sailing on *La Rueca*'s crew. It's all been a grand adventure, a fantasy I've been able to experience for a brief time, but I know it's not...real."

"The sailing has been real. Kissing you was—"

"Not real." If the kisses weren't real, neither were her feelings. "I mean, we kissed. But we were caught up in the moment. Two consenting adults in each other's arms. The opportunity presented itself. A kiss was bound to happen."

"Perhaps we should find out if the kisses are real or not."

Jules's gaze flew up to meet his.

His intense gaze seemed to penetrate all the way to

her soul. Her breath caught in her throat. She'd never felt so exposed, so naked before.

A chill rushed through her. Goose bumps prickled her skin. "We…can't."

"Why not?"

Her heart slammed against her chest. Logically she knew what she should say, but those words would contradict what her heart and her lips wanted her to do. "This can't go anywhere."

Alejandro traced her jawline with his fingertip. "I know."

His light-as-a-feather touch tantalized. Teased. Tempted. "I'm marrying Enrique."

"I know that, too." Alejandro's rich voice seeped into her, filling all the empty places with warmth. "The race begins tomorrow. This may be our last opportunity to be alone."

Jules's chest tightened. "This has to be the last time."

He nodded and lowered his hand from her face. "That would be for the best."

At least he agreed. Still, nerves gripped her. "But I…"

Silence hung between them, but instead of pushing them apart Alejandro drew closer. "Your move, Princess."

Her move. Jules had never been in this position before, but she knew what she had to do. She raised her chin and pressed her lips against his. Hard.

A mistake? Probably.

But she wanted—needed—to kiss him one more

time. She wanted to remember what his kiss felt like and how he made her feel.

Jules wrapped her arms around him and leaned in close. She tasted a mix of salt and heat. So delicious. She wanted to remember every detail, each texture.

As she deepened the kiss, sparks shot through her.

Okay, this kiss was real. She'd give him that.

The kiss made her quiver with pleasure and burn with desire.

But Jules didn't know if the way she felt was real or not. She didn't care. She just wanted to keep kissing him.

Because once she finished, Jules knew she would never kiss Alejandro again.

Tensions ran high the next morning. The first day of the Med Cup had arrived. Alejandro couldn't believe how calm and cool Julianna was. She impressed the entire crew with her composure. She steered like a pro. The entire team worked together. The sweat and hard work enabled *La Rueca* to win their first race. Alejandro's goal was one step closer.

And so was saying goodbye to Julianna.

He ignored the knot in his gut.

His father excused him from eating dinner at the palace that night. But Alejandro didn't feel like celebrating as he sat at a tapas bar with the crew so he headed back to the palace.

Julianna.

She should have been with the crew tonight. With him.

Alejandro wanted to take her in his arms and kiss her until she begged him to stop or give her more. But he couldn't.

This has to be the last time.

He'd agreed. Logically that made the most sense, but the way he felt about her didn't make sense at all.

The kitten was waiting when Alejandro entered the apartment. "Hey, Boots."

The kitten meowed.

Alejandro got an idea. "Want to go see Julianna?"

Another meow.

That was good enough for him. He swooped up the cat and went to Julianna's room.

In the hallway, Yvette sat on a chair outside the door and read. She lowered her book. "Are you here to see Princess Julianna, sir?"

"Yes." He showed her the kitten. "Boots wants to see her."

As if on cue, the cat meowed.

"I'm sorry, sir. The princess is sleeping."

Alejandro looked around. No one else was in the hallway. He smiled. "Please tell her I'm here."

"I'm sorry, sir," Yvette repeated with a hint of disapproval this time. "Princess Julianna has an upset stomach and asked not to be disturbed until morning. Would you like me to tell her you and Boots paid a visit?"

"No, thanks. I'll see her tomorrow." Disappointment

settled over the center of his chest. Alejandro wanted to see her now. "Good night."

He returned to his apartment feeling out of sorts. He played with Boots using the laser pointer, but the kitten had more fun.

The entire time, Alejandro couldn't stop thinking about Julianna. The passion in her eyes when they kissed. The exhilaration on her face during the race.

He had to see her for a minute. Yvette wasn't about to let him pass, but he knew another way.

With a flashlight in hand, Alejandro used the secret door in his apartment to enter the tunnels. He wove his way around until he reached the staircase leading to Julianna's room. Each step brought him closer to her. He stood on the landing and pulled the latch. The secret door opened.

Alejandro had been here before to leave her disguise and other gear she needed. He'd never thought twice about entering her closet.

But this time, he hesitated.

This can't go anywhere.

I know.

I'm marrying Enrique.

I know that, too.

His conversation with Julianna echoed through his head. Yes, he wanted to see her. Hell, he wanted to kiss her.

But Julianna didn't want that.

I'm marrying Enrique.

Alejandro might want to see her, but he couldn't.

She was determined to marry his brother. He wasn't going to do something that both he and Julianna might regret. He knew better than that.

Alejandro closed the secret door.

This was for the...best.

The morning of the race, Julianna had instructed Yvette to tell anyone who came to the door she was suffering from a stomach virus. No one, especially Enrique, would want any part of that.

Hours later, she stood with her hands on the wheel, nervous and excited. Adrenaline coursed through her veins.

They were halfway through the course, running ahead of their closest competitor.

The tension and noise level had increased from yesterday's match. The winds and waves had, too. Both had turned stronger over the last twenty-four hours. That made her job harder.

Water splashed into the cockpit. A foul weather suit kept her dry. Each member of the crew had a responsibility and knew what to do. Hers was to steer the boat. She focused her attention on the direction the boat sailed. She couldn't think about anything else.

Or anyone else.

But Jules knew where Alejandro had been since the boat had left the dock. Her gaze was automatically drawn to him at midbow. Water dripped from his hair and his foul weather gear. He looked sexy and in his element. The sheer joy on his face tugged on her heart and her dreams.

One more day of racing. A week until her wedding. And it would be all over.

A sense of loss assailed her. She ignored it. Now wasn't the time.

Each of the crew worked to keep the *La Rueca* sailing as fast as she could with adjustments to the sails. Others sat aft, trying to keep the weight on the stern.

The boat sailed downwind, surfing the waves that got bigger by the minute. The up and down motion of the boat reminded her of a thrilling roller coaster ride. More than once her stomach ended up in her throat, but she didn't mind one bit.

Jules tightened her grip on the wheel. She needed to hold a steady course, but didn't want to plow into a wave and risk the possibility of broaching.

Water hit her face and dripped down her cheeks. She tasted salt on her lips and in her mouth.

This was what she dreamed about. Freedom in its purest form.

She had no regrets. Well, one. Alejandro. But that wasn't as much a regret as a what-might-have-been. Kissing him again had left a wound on her heart. One she hoped would heal in time.

"*Dragon Rider*'s broached," Sam yelled from the midsection of the bow.

Jules could barely hear him, but she'd heard enough. Their competitor had heeled too far to one side and was lying broadside. Her stomach clenched.

She hoped the crew were tied in. It would be easy to capsize or break the mast in these waves.

Everyone searched for the boat. The sails and waves got in the way. The mast must be in the water or someone would see it.

"Does it look like they are going to recover?" Alejandro's voice sounded strained.

"I see them," Sam shouted.

"Me, too," Mike yelled. "They are knocked down."

Jules inhaled sharply, but held the course.

"Has the boat righted itself?" Phillipe, who was nearest to her, asked.

"No," Mike said.

The answer sent a chill down Jules's spine.

"Man overboard," a voice called over the radio.

"Trimming up for beam reaching," she said without a moment of hesitation.

Alejandro jumped off the deck and grabbed the radio. "*La Rueca* is responding."

The energy level tripled. A sailor was in the water. A life was at stake. The race no longer mattered. Every able-bodied vessel was required to offer assistance.

He looked at Jules. Confidence and affection shone in his eyes. "You can do this."

She nodded once.

As she turned the boat from the starboard side, the mainsail and jib trimmers went to work. No one wanted to waste any time, but they had to be careful. They didn't want to broach as well.

"Get a fix on the person in the water," she ordered Phillipe. With the race on hold, he needed another job. Jules needed to make sure she didn't run the sailor over.

"I've got the beacon," Alejandro said, moving toward the stern.

She knew he was clipped in, but she bit her lip, worried about his safety out there. And the other boat. They'd been fighting the waves all day. *If he went overboard...*

Don't think. Just steer.

"I see him," Mike yelled.

Jules heard the collective sigh of relief, but the sailor wasn't safe yet.

Alejandro threw the overboard buoy toward the sailor in the water. The buoy was state of the art with a lighted pole, life ring, flotation jacket and location beacon.

"Sailor has the beacon," Phillipe said. "You've sailed past him on the aft side."

"Coming about," she ordered. "Trim up."

Jules gave the second order even though it wasn't necessary. They knew what to do. She sailed over the waves. Tacking back, she guided the boat toward the buoy.

Alejandro stood on the bow, clipped into the jackline. Sam was nearby, too. They looked out at the water. Alejandro was too far away for her to hear him so he directed her with hand signals.

She slowed down, luffing leeward of the sailor in the water. The wind against the loose sails sounded like thunder. The crew shouted. The noise level kept rising. She must be getting closer.

Jules focused, pushing the boat to its limits to reach the sailor as quickly as possible.

A helicopter flew overhead.

Mike used a recovery hook to grab the buoy's line, pulling the buoy and the person toward them. Cody grabbed the buoy pole and dragged it back toward the stern.

"The other boat's righted," he said.

Thank goodness, but she couldn't celebrate yet. She kept the sails luffing so the boat wouldn't drift into the person bobbing in the water. Mike and Phillipe hauled the man onboard. His face was pale, but he looked relieved to be aboard. Water poured from his foul weather gear.

"We've got your sailor," Alejandro radioed. "But due to the weather conditions an exchange isn't possible."

"We're dropping out to recover," the voice replied.

Bummer, Jules thought. But two other boats were still racing. Her questioning gaze sought Alejandro's. He smiled at her, sending her heart into a pirouette.

"We'll keep going," he said over the radio.

"Thanks and good luck," the voice replied. "Tell your newest crew member to enjoy the ride."

"Will do," Alejandro said. "The extra weight will come in handy with these waves."

The guy on the radio laughed.

"Time to finish the race," Alejandro announced to the crew.

Everyone took his position with a cheer.

"We can win this." The confidence in Alejandro's voice kept her focused. "J.V."

"Coming about," she said.

It was as if the rescue had never happened. If not for their extra passenger it might have all been a dream.

But as they sailed toward the finish line, Jules knew it was real. Like Alejandro's kisses.

The bow crossed the finish line.

The crew cheered. Jules laughed.

They'd won.

Won!

La Rueca would be in the finals tomorrow.

Excitement rocketed through her. She stared at Alejandro. A grin lit up his face. So handsome. So dear to her heart.

He gave her a high-five. She would have preferred a hug, but being able to touch him was enough. For now.

"I've never seen anyone sail like you did today," he said. "Awe-inspiring."

"You're the best, J.V.," Sam said.

"Thanks for the ride." The sailor they'd rescued, Robert, shook her hand. "We underestimated you, kid. You're one helluva a helmsman."

Jules smiled, but didn't say anything. Her voice would give her away. She couldn't fake a deep tone now. Not with delighted joy exploding like fireworks in her chest.

The boat docked. People were waiting for them. A medical crew stood in front of the crowd.

"Looks like you'll need a checkup," Alejandro said to their guest.

Robert had changed into spare dry clothes down below. "I'd rather hit the bar and wait for my boat to arrive."

"Maybe there's a pretty doc or nurse to keep you company, mate," Sam said.

"One can hope." Robert saluted Jules and the rest of the crew. "Thanks again. Good race, but watch out for us next year."

Alejandro laughed. "We'll have our eyes open looking back at you the entire way."

Robert grinned wryly. "With this kid driving, you might be."

As he left with the medical crew, people pushed forward.

"Look at all these fans, mates," Sam said. "Smile. The media is here, too."

Jules's heart slammed against her chest. A horrible sense of dread replaced the wonderfulness of the moment. The press took pictures, asked questions, followed up.

So not good.

She ducked her head and pulled her cap lower.

"You may find yourself a pretty girl out of this, J.V.," Sam teased with a slap on Jules's back.

Jules forced a smile. Anything would be better than the truth coming out.

"Don't worry," Alejandro whispered so only she could hear.

She appreciated his words, but she was worried.

Terrified. Her future, her country's future and her children's future were all at stake. The press circled like a school of hungry piranhas. She swallowed around the spinnaker-size lump in her throat.

The sea of people standing on the dock grew larger. Some held cameras. A few shouted questions in a variety of languages: Spanish, German, French, Italian and English. She understood most of the questions, but she pretended not to hear them.

Her insides trembled, but she maintained her composure. A teenage boy would relish the attention after winning a race, not run away. Still her feet were itching to take off.

Who was she kidding?

If she could jump into the water and swim away without drawing attention to herself, she would.

"We need to get you out of here," Alejandro whispered.

"I can swim."

"So can the sharks." He tried to lead her away from the mob, but the crowd pushed closer. "It'll be okay."

She clung to his words even though her doubts multiplied by the seconds. Camera flashes blinded her. Reporters shoved microphones and digital recorders in her face. Arms reached for her.

Jules cringed. Bodyguards never let crowds get so close. She wasn't used to being touched like this. Her anxiety level spiraled.

Someone touched her cap.

"Please don't." She held it on her head with both hands. "Alejandro."

He tried to help her. "Leave the kid alone."

Another person grabbed the cap off her head. The wig went with it, leaving her wearing a nylon cap.

People gasped. A horrible silence fell over the crowd.

"It's a girl," a man shouted.

"A woman," another yelled.

"Hey," a woman said. "Isn't that the princess who's going to marry Crown Prince Enrique?"

The air rushed from her lungs. Her worst nightmare was coming true. Everyone would know her true identity now. Including Enrique and her father.

Her heart and her head felt as if they might explode.

Hundreds of people surrounded her, but she'd never felt so alone. And she had only herself to blame.

Life as she knew it was over.

Had it been worth it?

She glanced at Alejandro. He'd removed his sunglasses. The warmth in his eyes drove her goose bumps away.

"Do not worry," he said softly. "I'm here. You won't have to face this alone."

His words gave her the strength she needed. She knew sailing with Alejandro had been worth it. No matter what the consequences.

Shoulders back. Chin up. Smile.

Jules fell back into the training that had been ingrained in her since she was a little girl. She removed the plastic cap hiding her blond hair.

Goodbye J.V., hello Princess Julianna.

She answered the questions being shouted at her. Alejandro stood next to her the entire time. He downplayed the situation by answering questions as well. She appreciated his efforts. The rest of the crew stayed by her, too, though they looked confused. Phillipe's brows furrowed. Mike's mouth gaped. Cody scratched his head. Sam stared at her as if she were a ghost.

But Alejandro's presence gave her strength. Courage.

A good thing, too. When her father and her fiancé discovered what Jules had done, she was going to need all that and more.

CHAPTER TWELVE

BACK AT THE PALACE, Jules couldn't stop shaking. Not even a hot shower helped. She put on a conservative pink dress, befitting a princess and future queen. With trembling hands, she applied makeup and styled her hair in an updo.

What was her father going to say? Do about her disobedience?

Yvette fastened a strand of pearls around Jules's neck. "You look like a proper princess, ma'am."

She hadn't been acting like one. "Thank you."

A knock sounded on her door. Jules's heart pounded in her ears. She wasn't ready.

Yvette answered the door. "It's Prince Brandt, ma'am. He's here to escort you to the sitting room."

As soon as Jules stepped into the hallway, her brother hugged her. "Father requests your presence."

She stepped out of Brandt's embrace. "Yvette said he arrived like a bull from Pamplona. Snorts and all."

"I've never seen him so angry." The concern in Brandt's voice matched her own. "I'm worried what he'll do."

She wanted to ease Brandt's concern even though she was apprehensive, too. "Don't worry. Father will be...fair."

At least she hoped so.

"I screwed up." Brandt hung his head. "Klaus is beside himself for leaving you alone so much."

Jules touched her brother's shoulder. Love for him filled her heart. "Neither of you are to blame for this."

Only her.

She descended the stairs, mindful of each step so she didn't stumble.

"But if I hadn't been partying so much—"

"Please, Brandt." Straightening, Jules composed herself. She couldn't duck for cover now. "Don't get in the middle of this."

It would be bad enough without dragging him or Alejandro into this.

Alejandro.

His name brought a welcome rush of warmth through her cold body. She'd survived the onslaught of questions on the dock with him at her side. If she had the same help tonight...

No, that was too much to ask of him. Her father was too rich, too powerful. He could destroy everything Alejandro worked so hard to build.

The sitting room loomed in front of her like a black hole. She entered with Brandt at her side.

A tense silence filled the air. Alejandro, Enrique King Dario and her father rose from their seats.

Compassion filled Alejandro's eyes. He'd shaved

emoved his earring and pulled his hair away from his ace and secured it at his nape. He looked regal and princely in his suit, dress shirt, tie and leather shoes. Respectable. Her heart squeezed tight. She missed he pirate.

Enrique had dressed similarly. The two men had never looked as much like brothers as tonight. Enrique glared at Alejandro with accusation and a frown on his lips.

She hated knowing she would push the two men farther apart.

Concern clouded King Dario's face. He pressed his lips together and clasped his hands behind his back. Sweat beaded on his brow.

Her father's gaze burned with fury. His lips thinned with anger. "How dare you disobey me, Julianna Louise Marie!"

Shoulders back. Chin up.

No way could she smile. Jules looked him in he eyes. She wanted to be strong for Brandt's and Alejandro's sake, as much as her own. "I apologize for my actions, sir. I didn't mean to cause any trouble."

"Trouble?" Alaric's features hardened. "You have brought disrepute onto our family and country. Pictures of you looking windswept and wild, hardly he way a princess should appear in public, are everywhere. Papers, television, the Internet."

Jules felt everyone's eyes on her, especially Alejandro's. She tried not to cower, but she'd never seen her father so full of rage.

Enrique sneered. "You looked like a boy."

"It was a disguise," she explained, cutting him with a quick glance.

"The fact you needed a disguise should have been the first sign this was a mistake." King Dario patted his forehead with his handkerchief. "You're the future queen of La Isla de la Aurora, Julianna. This kind of behavior is unacceptable."

"I'll say." Enrique glowered at her. "Your father and I told you not to sail. You're supposed to be a conservative princess. Not a...wild child."

Her temper rose. "I wasn't—"

"You were." Her father's voice boomed like a thunderstorm in November. "I watched a tape of the race on the flight. You not only disobeyed me but put yourself in danger. You could have been killed sailing the way you did today."

Heat stole into her face. Her breath burned in her throat.

"Jules is fine, Father. She saved a sailor's life," Brandt said bravely. He'd never stood up to their father before and she was proud he'd found the courage to do that. "It's my fault Klaus wasn't with Jules. I partied too much, and he was with me."

Her muscles tensed, nervous what her father would say.

"This has nothing to do with you, Brandt," Alaric replied sharply. "Your sister knew what I expected of her. She must accept the consequences."

Dread shuddered through her. Jules knew what her punishment would be—to spend the rest of her life in Aliestle.

She glanced at Alejandro. Her heart cried. She would never see him again.

"King Alaric." Alejandro stepped forward. "I am Prince Alejandro Cierzo de Amanecer. King Dario's second son."

"You mean, the spare." King Alaric's curt voice lashed out. "You're the idiot who put my daughter's life in danger."

Jules drew in a sharp breath at the insult. She couldn't stand the thought of her father taking out his anger on Alejandro.

"Yes, but Julianna's safety is of the utmost concern to me, Your Majesty." The regal air emanating from him made him seem more like a future king than second in line for the throne. "I take full responsibility for what's happened. Julianna disobeying you was one hundred percent my fault. I took her sailing. I asked her to be part of my crew and race in the Med Cup. I'm the one who should be punished, not her."

Jules stared at Alejandro, full of pride and…love. *I love him.*

Love was the only explanation for her feelings, ones that went far deeper than friendship and future familial bonds. She couldn't stop thinking about the way he looked at her, kissed her, stood by her side and wanted to take the blame for all of this.

Alejandro had to have feelings for her. Otherwise why would he be standing up for her now? Her heart wanted her to go to him, but too many things needed to be resolved first.

Jules couldn't allow Alejandro to take the blame.

She hadn't been a dutiful princess. She'd disobeyed. She needed to stand up and be accountable for her actions, not let a wonderful, giving man suffer consequences meant for her.

Joy provided strength. Love gave her courage.

Alejandro embraced his role as a prince tonight to protect her. She needed to embrace her role as a black sheep to accept her punishment and protect him.

"Thank you, Alejandro." An unfamiliar sense of peace rested in her heart. "But I can't allow you take the blame for my actions."

His eyes implored her. "It's my blame to take."

Her heart melted. She allowed her gaze to linger, longer than what was considered proper. She loved the gold flecks and the concern she saw in his brown eyes. "No."

"Yes," Enrique countered. "All this is Alejandro's fault, King Alaric."

"It's not. I knew what I was getting myself into, Father." Jules stared up at her father, who towered over her with a face full of contempt. "I was so desperate for a taste of freedom, I allowed my desire to override everything else. Alejandro's not to blame. It's my fault. But I have no regrets over what I have done."

The affection and pride in Alejandro's eyes made her heart want to dance and sing. Whatever consequence she faced would be worth it. If she hadn't disobeyed, she would never have gotten to know him, kiss him and fall in love with him.

"Your stepmother worked so hard to turn you into

a proper Aliestlian princess." Her father spoke with disdain. "But you have always been too much like your mother."

Jules smiled. "Thank you, Father."

His nostrils flared. "It isn't a compliment."

Her smile didn't waver. She would cherish the words no matter what fate had in store for her. "It is to me, sir."

The wrinkles on her father's forehead deepened. He stared at her with a look of bewilderment then turned his attention to King Dario. "I trusted you with my most prized possession. You promised she would be safe, yet you allowed this to happen."

"We had no idea she was sailing." King Dario sounded contrite.

"Her well-being is our number one priority," Enrique added.

Jules hated how they spoke as if she wasn't present. "I'm right here, gentlemen."

Alaric ignored her. "If that's the case, how come no one noticed she was missing from the palace? Not even her fiancé?"

"I've been busy with work and wedding plans," Enrique answered hastily.

Alaric's lips snarled. "Wedding plans are women's work."

Enrique flinched.

"My brother had no idea because he works nonstop as crown prince. He would have no reason to suspect anything was amiss because Julianna didn't allow the sailing to affect her obligations as his fiancée," Alejandro explained. "There was no harm done."

"No harm?" Her father's ruddy complexion reddened more. "Her blatant disobedience has thrown Aliestle into chaos. A small feminist movement has taken her participation in the race and run with it. They are holding rallies across the land and protesting for equal rights. It's disgusting."

No, it was progress. The kind of change Jules wanted to influence in her country. Satisfaction flowed through her.

Approval gleamed in Alejandro's eyes. He knew what this meant to her.

She smiled at him.

He smiled back.

"This situation is completely out of hand and unacceptable," Alaric announced. "I'm canceling the marriage contract."

Panic clawed into her heart. Jules didn't want to return to Aliestle. She wanted to stay on the island with Alejandro.

What now? Did she dare defy her father again?

As the king's words echoed through the room, Alejandro stared at Julianna. The distress on her face twisted his insides.

Emotions clamored in his heart, demanding to be acknowledged. Not respect or attraction or friendship. Deep feelings. Intense feelings. Ones that scared him.

Not love. He knew better than to fall in love. This had to be…something else.

Still his hand itched to reach out to take hold of Julianna. He wanted to protect her from the fallout and make everything better.

Brandt cleared his throat. "Father, please—"

"This does not concern you," Alaric said through clenched teeth.

But it concerned Alejandro. He wanted to punch King Alaric in the nose and free her from this tyranny. But that wasn't what Julianna wanted him to do. And it certainly wouldn't help her with her father. In fact, acting out the fury balling in his gut would cause more trouble for his own family.

Alejandro's frustration rose.

If she returned to Aliestle, her sense of duty would lead her to marry whatever nobleman her father picked out.

Alejandro couldn't allow that to happen. She had to stay on the island. No matter what. "Your Majesty, if I may…"

King Alaric glared at him. "Haven't you done enough already?"

"Sire." The old-fashioned word felt weird coming off Alejandro's tongue, but perhaps it would resonate with the misguided and medieval King Alaric. "Julianna needs to remain on La Isla de la Aurora."

"Why?" Scorn laced King Alaric's word.

"Because I want to stay here, Father," Julianna said.

She smiled softly at Alejandro.

His heart turned over. And that hurt like hell because to do the right thing, he had to let her go.

"The people are wild about her, sire." Alejandro had been in his brother's shadow his entire life, but this time he belonged there. Only Enrique could give Julianna the kind of life she was raised for, the kind of life she wanted. She wanted to use her position as the crown prince's wife to influence change and give her people a better future. She could accomplish all she desired and more as the future queen. "Julianna has touched their hearts with her compassion and friendliness. They've embraced her as their princess, and one day they'll love her as their queen."

"My daughter was raised to be a queen," Alaric admitted.

"Everyone can tell she has received the finest training." Alejandro fought the desire to claim her for himself. But too much was at stake. He could never give Julianna what she wanted and make her happy, even if she wished to be with him. He swallowed around the lump of emotion in his throat. He had to push aside his own desire and do what was best for her. "You say her actions have caused chaos, sire. But her countrywomen see someone they can relate to and rally around. A respected and beloved leader. As the future queen of La Isla de la Aurora, Julianna will be able to do that for women not only in Aliestle and here on the island, but all over the world."

"Please consider my youngest son's words." Appreciation gleamed in Dario's eyes. "Alejandro may not be a conventional prince, but he is wise for his age and speaks the truth."

That was the first compliment his father had ever

given him. And the words couldn't have come at a better time.

"Julianna has enchanted the entire island," Enrique added. "And all of us."

Especially Alejandro. But his feelings didn't matter. Julianna would get what she wanted and by default, so would he. He wanted freedom from the monarchy, not a princess bride who dreamed of happily ever afters.

His thoughts tasted like ashes in his mouth. But he had to be realistic. He didn't want to be a prince. He avoided romantic entanglements like the plague. It would...never work.

King Alaric looked at each one of them, but his assessing gaze lingered on Alejandro. "So it seems."

"I stand by the marriage contract," Enrique announced. "I want to marry Julianna."

Her face showed no change of emotion, but his brother's words crushed into Alejandro like a left hook. He resisted the urge not to carry her off to his boat and sail away. But he was the second son, the spare. He wasn't what Julianna needed.

"I don't know." King Alaric's gaze bounced between Alejandro and Julianna. "There seems to be a strong...connection between these two."

"Friendship, sire." Enrique sidled closer to Julianna, as if to reclaim his prize. "They both enjoy sailing."

Alaric looked doubtful.

Perceptive man, Alejandro had to admit. Other

than passion, there wasn't anything binding him to Julianna. There couldn't be. "We are friends, sire."

"There will be complications if Julianna has done more than sail with her friend Alejandro," Alaric said. "If there is any reason to doubt the paternity of an heir, the embarrassment to our family name…"

Julianna flushed.

Anger surged. Alejandro couldn't believe her father was questioning her virginity. He balled his hands into fists. "I assure you, sir—"

King Alaric cut him off. He stared at his daughter as if she were a peasant, not a princess. "Is there any reason you shouldn't marry Enrique?"

The question mortified Julianna. Her heart pounded in her chest, so loudly she was certain everyone could hear it. But no one said anything. They stared, waiting for her to answer.

Her father with his dark, accusing eyes.

King Dario with compassion.

Enrique with panic.

And Alejandro with hope.

Is there any reason you shouldn't marry Enrique?

Yes, a big reason. A six-foot-two-inch-tall reason with dark hair and dark eyes.

Alejandro.

Jules loved him, but couldn't understand why he kept talking about her being a future queen. She wanted to stay on the island, but with Alejandro, not his brother.

She made a silent wish from her heart.

Claim me.

Jules wanted Alejandro to forget about everything. His family, her family and their two countries. She wanted him to declare his love and claim her for himself.

Alejandro gave her an encouraging smile filled with warmth.

Relief washed over her. Her tense muscles relaxed. He would come to her rescue once again and claim her. Everything would turn out fine.

"You can still do your duty and help your country," Alejandro insisted. "All you have to do is tell your father that marrying Enrique is what you want."

Emotion tightened her throat. Her body stiffened with shock.

No. She didn't want that. She loved Alejandro. His actions told her he had feelings for her, too.

There was something between them. Something special.

Yet he wanted her to marry his brother. Jules struggled to breathe. She stared at him.

His smile disappeared. His expression turned neutral.

Why was he doing this?

And then something clicked in her mind and she remembered...

Once you and Enrique marry and have children, I'll be free from all royal obligations. I can concentrate on business and not have to worry about any more princely duties.

The truth hit her with stark clarity. She didn't want to believe it, but nothing else made sense.

Alejandro might have feelings for her, but the feelings didn't run deep enough. He chose not to act upon them. He wasn't willing to sacrifice what he wanted. His freedom was more important than duty. Love. Her.

Julianna's heart froze, leaving her feeling cold and empty.

Despair threatened to overwhelm her, but she didn't give in to it. She needed to answer her father's question.

A million thoughts jumbled her mind. But one kept coming back to her. Her actions on the island had created the very sort of change she desired in Aliestle.

Was that enough reason to marry Enrique?

She looked at Brandt. If she didn't go through with the wedding now, the repercussions would reflect badly on her brother. He was the one who was supposed to be escorting her safely to marriage. The Council of Elders would blame him, so would the press. Their plans to help their country would never come to fruition if she returned home.

Before Alejandro and getting caught up in a fantasy, she'd had a plan—a life outside of Aliestle, helping Brandt and her country, falling in love with her husband and becoming a mother. She might not achieve all of those things now, but she could have some of them.

That would have to be enough.

Shoulders back. Chin up. Smile.

"There isn't any reason I shouldn't marry Enrique, Father." Jules sneaked a peek at Alejandro. The gold flecks in his eyes burned like flames. Somehow she would have to learn to live with Enrique as her husband and Alejandro as her brother-in-law. And be satisfied with that. She swallowed a sigh. "No reason at all."

"I am satisfied." Alaric proclaimed after a long minute. "The marriage contract will be honored, provided Julianna not sail in the Med Cup tomorrow. I'll be here to see to it that she remains in the palace all day long."

Every one of her nerve endings cried out in protest. Jules had earned the spot in the final, but she remained silent as any proper princess would.

"As will I," King Dario said.

"Me, too," Enrique agreed.

Alejandro nodded. "Julianna is a skilled helmsman, but I agree it's best she doesn't sail."

Even he was taking their side. Her heart shattered into a million pieces, each one jabbing into her at the same time. If love and passion brought this kind of pain, she would rather go back to how she lived before arriving on the island.

With what strength she had left, Jules forced all her emotions to a deep, dark place. She'd survived before by sleepwalking through life. That was how she would survive again.

The dullness in Julianna's eyes struck at Alejandro's heart. He knew she was upset at being banned from the race. Competing in the Med Cup had been important to her. At least she was getting what she wanted. She could help her brother and her country now.

But the lack of emotion on her face and her lifeless eyes bothered him. Concerned, he turned toward her. "Jul—"

"There's no reason for you to remain at the palace, Alejandro." King Dario interrupted him with a pointed glare. "Return to your villa and prepare for tomorrow's race."

Alejandro didn't want to leave. He wanted to stay near Julianna. "I don't mind staying here."

"Go." His father touched his shoulder. "Keep your distance until the wedding."

Julianna didn't glance Alejandro's way. He knew why.

She'd put her princess mask back on.

He wanted to reach out to her, to shake some sense into her, but he couldn't. He'd pushed aside his own feelings to help her be a proper princess again. A mistake, probably.

But that was what she needed. More than she needed him.

Alejandro had to let Julianna go so she could fulfill the royal duty that was so important to her. She wouldn't disappear from his life. She would disappear into being his distant sister-in-law. Thinking about it now, having her leave the island might have been easier to deal with.

"Perhaps you should stay away after the wedding

too," King Alaric said. "I'll see to it you're well compensated, Alejandro."

His temper flared. He wasn't about to allow Julianna's father to pay him off to stay away. "That isn't necessary, sir. I know my place."

"You're now free from your royal obligations, my son," Dario announced. "I know this is what you've always wanted."

Alejandro nodded. But he didn't feel any relief. No happiness. "Thank you, Father."

He'd gotten what he set out to get—his freedom. He'd never have to step back inside the palace or appear at openings, dinners or charity events. He was free to live his life as he wanted—building boats, racing and turning around the island's economy. No more royal orders. No more royal interference.

But it felt...anticlimactic. Wrong.

Julianna moved closer to Enrique.

Sharp pain sliced Alejandro. A black void seemed to engulf his heart. Seeing her so willingly embrace her future with Enrique shouldn't hurt so badly.

Alejandro shook off the feeling. He was jealous and feeling guilty for what he'd done. That was all.

Enrique had won again. No doubt his brother would punish him for going behind his back.

"Under the circumstances," Enrique said. "I do not think it wise for you to be my best man."

"I agree." Alejandro looked at Julianna. "You're the best helmsman I've had the privilege of sailing with. You'll be missed."

"Thank you for allowing me to sail on your boat." She spoke politely as if he were some hired help.

The ice princess had returned. But he knew she wasn't cold and heartless, but warm and genuine. He wanted to rip the mask off her face so he could see the real Julianna.

"Good luck with the race tomorrow," she added.

She'd earned *La Rueca* the spot in the finals tomorrow. But she had known her father would never allow her sailing to continue once the truth was out.

"I know you want to sail, Julianna," Alejandro said. "But it's best if you resume your life and do what is best for your country and mine. I don't see any other—"

"No explanations are needed, sir." She emphasized the last word with a haughtiness that put him in his place. "I know my duty. I always have. I was using you as a means to an end, one last hurrah before settling into the life I've chosen. No hard feelings, right?"

Each of her words pierced his heart like a dagger. He had hard feelings, ones that were becoming difficult to ignore and fight.

Using him? Okay, he'd used her to do well in the race.

Alejandro hated to think what she said was true. They'd shared good times, their hopes and their dreams, and hot kisses. Maybe she didn't have feelings for him or maybe she was back to pretending. It didn't matter.

The next time he saw her, they would be required

to wear polite faces and share a meaningless conversation. Everything in the past would seem like nothing more than a dream.

No hard feelings, right?

"Right." Alejandro bowed. "I wish you much happiness. All of you."

With that, he packed his bag, picked up Boots and left the palace feeling worse than he'd ever felt in his entire life.

CHAPTER THIRTEEN

THE TWO KINGS, satisfied to have the marriage between their children moving forward, retired to the library to have a brandy. Jules sat in the sitting room with Enrique. He'd wanted to talk with her alone. She didn't blame him. She figured he wanted to talk about his brother.

Alejandro.

Her heart ached.

Who was she kidding?

She felt as if her heart died when Alejandro left. The raw hurt in his eyes made it hard for her to breathe. She'd hurt him with her words. Worse, she'd done it on purpose. She'd lashed out in her own hurt because he'd been unwilling to make a commitment to her.

She wanted to scream and cry, but instead she sat showing no emotion on her face. The way she'd done her entire life, except for the time she'd spent with Alejandro. Sailing, talking, building castles in the sand.

The best time of her life.

Don't think about him. As he'd said, she had to resume her life...

"I understand how easy it must have been to get carried away with the sailing, but I must know..." Enrique rose from the damask-covered settee. He stood in front of her, towering over her while she remained seated. His mouth narrowed into a thin line. "Did you have sex with my brother?"

It wasn't as much a question as a demand. An easy one to answer, but she hesitated.

Jules knew her life on the island would be better than life in Aliestle, but not by much. Enrique would see to that. He only cared about himself. She would always be an extension of his persona to be controlled so she wouldn't embarrass him.

She stood and raised her chin. "I didn't have sex with Alejandro."

The tension on Enrique's face disappeared.

"But I'm in love with him," she admitted.

"I'm not surprised." Enrique sounded more amused than angry. "Alejandro has seduced many beautiful women and left a trail of broken hearts on this island. Someone as innocent as you never stood a chance. Do not worry. Once we're married, you'll forget him."

Surprise echoed through her. "You still want to marry me knowing I love another man?"

"Of course," Enrique said. "I thought he might have wanted sex from you. I realize he wanted to win the race so he could promote his business. But now that he received so much publicity today, winning the race, and therefore you, are no longer necessary."

His words took the wind out of her sails. "I'm a necessary part of his crew."

Enrique shrugged. "If that's true, why didn't he argue to have you race with him tomorrow?"

Feeling like she'd hit a reef and was taking on water fast, she struggled to breathe. To think. "Because of my father. And you."

"Believe that if it makes you feel better, but one day you'll realize the truth."

Jules knew the truth. Alejandro had told her it himself.

If La Rueca places in the top five, the resulting publicity will boost my boatyard's reputation and raise the island's standing in the eyes of the yachting world. To do that I need you steering the boat.

She narrowed her gaze. "Your brother wanted me so he could win the race. And you want me for my dowry."

Enrique grinned wryly. "Your royal bloodline doesn't hurt."

The two brothers were similar. Both men were selfish.

The realization hit her full force, the pain soul-deep.

But she couldn't entirely blame Alejandro for pursuing the freedom she was too scared to reach for herself.

She had let him go, but she couldn't let herself go. Surrendering and being obedient wasn't going to bring real change and happiness. She had to find her own path like Alejandro had done.

Effecting change meant not passively waiting and hoping, but required real, risk-taking leadership. The women's rights rallies weren't occuring because she'd been a dutiful princess, but because she'd been a defiant one who sailed in a race like her mother.

If she married Enrique, she would perpetuate the same repression her father had returned to in the wake of her mother's death. Jules wouldn't be an example for change, but of the status quo.

She'd been sleepwalking through life out of duty, but there was a higher duty: to be true to one's self.

However much we love people or have loved them, we still have to be the person we are meant to be.

Alejandro had been talking about his family when he'd spoken those words to her. Jules hadn't realized how much the words spoke to her soul until now.

Being true to one's self had more power to improve lives than she realized. Alejandro had taught her that. And she wanted to teach that to any children she had, both sons and daughters.

It was time for her to wake up for good. She needed to stand up for herself and go after what she wanted. She wanted to be the person her mother wanted her to be, the kind of person the women of Aliestle could be proud of.

She squared her shoulders. "La Isla de la Aurora might be more progressive, but you and Alejandro are as selfish as the men in Aliestle. Neither of you value women for who they are, but for what they can provide you."

"Why are you so surprised?" Enrique asked. "You

agreed to an arranged marriage. Did you think this would turn into a love match?"

"Yes. I hoped it would." Ridiculous fantasy that it was. "Like my parents' arranged marriage."

Enrique laughed. "Love is a childish notion that royalty cannot indulge in."

His words strengthened her. "I appreciate you wanting to marry me, but I can't marry you. I ask to be released from our arrangement."

His eyes flared with surprise. "Because of Alejandro."

"No. He doesn't want me." The knowledge bit into her, but she refused to give it any measure. She'd awoken to possibilities thanks to Alejandro for which she would always be grateful. "But that doesn't mean I can't find love, a real love I can count on."

"What have you done?" King Alaric looked as if one of the blood vessels in his forehead might burst. "You march back in there and tell Enrique you were mistaken."

"I'm not mistaken about this, Father." All she'd learned while on this island paradise empowered her. "Enrique only wants my dowry."

"So?"

She boldly met her father's gaze. "So I want more from a marriage than that."

"You'll see what you end up with when we return home and you marry an Aliestlian."

His words unleashed something deep inside of her, something lying dormant for too long. "I'm not returning to Aliestle," she said with a new sense of conviction. "I'm not going to be forced into a marriage I don't want."

"This is your duty."

"Perhaps once, but no longer. I believe my mother would've understood."

"I will not stand for this impertinence." He stood, his nostrils flaring. "You will obey me or I will disown you. You will lose your title, your home, your allowance. I will strip you of your passport. You will have nothing left. No money. No home. No country."

The thought of losing everything hurt, but she had to follow her own path. Her own heart. Jules didn't need to be claimed by a man or rescued. She could take care of herself. "If that is what you must do, Father, go ahead."

"You are dead to me," he screamed.

Tears stung her eyes. She felt an odd mix of sadness and joy. But she held firm. For the first time in her life, she was completely free of duty. Until now, everything in her life had been planned out, dictated by others. "Father..."

He turned his back on her.

She would have to make her own way, create a new life for herself. She was in charge now. She got to decide who she would be.

But Jules already knew.

She was like her mother, Queen Brigitta. Jules was a sailor, and a sailor sailed. She needed to get back into the Med Cup race even if Alejandro didn't want her. She needed to do it for herself, her mother and for all the women in Aliestle.

"I'll always love you, Father."

And she walked out of the room to an uncertain future.

Alejandro barely slept. Early the next morning, he wandered through his villa, unable to shake his uneasiness and loneliness. Strange, given he was back home, free to race and do as he pleased.

Boots meowed, sounding sad as if he knew Julianna and her treats were gone.

Gone.

He'd let Julianna go so she could be happy. Now he was miserable.

Alejandro dragged his hand through his hair. He missed her already. He'd done everything on his own for so long and been self-reliant, but this past week and a half, he'd been in a partnership. One, he realized now, he didn't want to end.

Everything in his life—Boots, *La Rueca* and his plans for the island—had become built around Julianna. He cared what she thought about things. He valued her opinion. He was happier than he'd ever been when he was with her. She was happy, too.

That had to count for something.

Would it be enough?

He hoped so because he realized that he was willing to fight for it. For her.

Letting Julianna go had been the wrong decision. One he regretted with his whole heart. Somehow he had to show her happiness and love were as important as her sense of duty.

I love her.

His heart pounded a ferocious beat. Feelings he'd tried to ignore burst to the surface. He staggered back until he hit the wall.

Alejandro wasn't sure when it had happened, sailing or on the beach, but he loved Julianna. Body, heart and soul. He loved the way she could be so prim and proper, but yearn for adventure at the same time. He loved the way she sailed as if her life depended on it. He loved her smile, her laughter and her tears. He loved the way she made him want to be a better man.

He struggled to breathe.

Love might not always last, but they weren't his parents. Julianna was too important not to at least try. The life Alejandro wanted wasn't going to work unless she was a part of it.

"I've got to go after her," he said to Boots. "I have to convince her we have a future together."

Boots meowed.

Alejandro ran out the villa's front door.

The sun rose as he drove up the windy road to the palace. No red sky this morning, just golden-yellow and orange rays. The beginning of a beautiful day, he hoped.

The only other car on the road was his security detail following him. No matter what time of day, they were always right there behind him. His father must have forgotten to tell them their services were no longer required.

Inside the palace, he ran through the hallway to her room. Yvette wasn't sitting outside.

He knocked.

No one answered.

He knocked again.

"She's not here." Enrique slurred the words. He wore the same clothes as last night sans jacket and held a bottle of wine. "Julianna broke off the match. Alaric disowned her. She's gone."

Alejandro's heart soared. If Julianna called off the wedding and gave up on doing her duty, that might mean she loved him. If she didn't, he'd show her the feelings between them were real. "Where is she?"

"What is all the noise?" His father walked down the hallway in his robe and slippers. "Do you know what time it is?"

Enrique burped. "His fault."

"Where is Julianna, Father?" Alejandro asked.

"I don't know," Dario admitted. "I offered to let her stay in the palace until she sorted things out, but she said it was time for her to start doing things on her own."

"Is Klaus with her?"

"King Alaric forbid the bodyguard from going with her," Dario said. "I thought Klaus was going to cry. Brandt is with him now."

"Yvette?"

"She broke down." Dario shook his head. "Elena is with her."

"I must find Julianna, Father. I need to know she's safe." Alejandro had spent much of his life rebelling and retreating from his duty, wanting to be alone and doing everything himself. But not today. "I love her. I need to tell her that even if she doesn't feel the same way."

"She's an ice princess." Enrique swaggered down the hallway. "All that money gone. Gone. Gone."

"Alaric took away Julianna's passport so she's on the island," Dario said in earnest to Alejandro.

"It's a start." But where on the island would she go? She didn't know anyone that well.

His father placed a hand on Alejandro's shoulder. "I was wrong trying to control everyone. That is what drove your mother away. I didn't want to lose you, too, so I wouldn't allow her to take you. But I fear I have lost you anyway, Alejandro. We don't always see eye to eye, but I hope you know I love you and am proud of the man you've become."

Alejandro choked up. That was all he'd ever wanted from his father. "I love you, too."

"We'll have to start listening to each other as a family. Perhaps you can show me your plans for the properties you've purchased."

Alejandro nodded.

His father smiled. "Good luck with Julianna, son."

"Thanks." Alejandro ran to his car. The island wasn't that big, but searching for her alone would take too much time. The crew was preparing for the race.

The race.

No, Julianna was more important.

He saw a familiar car and sprinted over to his security detail. "We must find Princess Julianna. I don't care if you have to search every single hotel on the island. Find her."

For the next two hours, Alejandro searched to no avail. He checked the tunnels, the beach, the dock and the yacht club that was sponsoring the race. The narrow streets grew crowded as the town came alive. Excitement about the Med Cup finals filled the air.

Text messages from the crew asking where he was and why he wasn't at the boat preparing for the race, grew more frantic. They also wanted to know if J.V. was coming.

Alejandro didn't want them to know Julianna was missing. He finally sent a reply he never expected to send: Go without me.

He'd regret not looking for Julianna more than he'd regret missing the race.

The race.

He'd checked the yacht club earlier, but she might go to the boat to race.

Hope glimmered, the first time all morning.

Traffic clogged the roads. Impatient, Alejandro parked on the side of the road, exited the car and jogged to the marina.

Up ahead, a woman with long, blond hair wearing the colors of his crew headed toward the yacht club.

"Julianna," he yelled.

She didn't stop. Alejandro ran after her, but was

going against the crowd of people. He found himself being pushed back.

He had to reach her somehow.

Alejandro saw a narrow opening between buildings. He worked his way over, but a large hedge blocked his way.

Nothing was going to stop him from reaching her.

Looking around, he saw a crate. He dragged it over and climbed over the hedge. His team jacket caught on a thorn and tore. He didn't care. He dropped down on the other side, jumped over some small plants until he made it to a paved walkway that led to the marina.

Alejandro ran, his legs pumping as fast as they could, but he'd lost sight of her. Julianna was… gone.

A bolt of grief ripped through him. His fault. He had no one else to blame.

He stared at the marina in the distance. A familiar mast caught his attention. *La Rueca* was heading out to the course to race.

Alejandro didn't know whether to laugh or cry. He pulled out his phone instead.

Good luck, he texted.

Sam replied: We've got J.V., no luck needed.

Alejandro read the message three times before the words sunk in. Julianna *had* been on her way to *La Rueca*. She'd made it onboard in time.

But he hadn't.

He laughed.

Now he would have to wait to see how things turned out both with *La Rueca* and Julianna. But at least he knew she was safe. That was enough. For now.

He texted Sam, asking him to hand his mobile phone to Julianna.

What? she asked.

He typed, You OK?

OK. You?

Alejandro typed a message and hit Send.

That was all he could do now.

He called his security detail and his father then made his way to the yacht club. There, he could watch the race unfold. His boat was out there with the woman he loved at the helm. He didn't want to miss a single minute of it.

The race was in its final leg. Not having Alejandro aboard was strange, especially during such a tight race. *La Rueca* had made up distance since heading upwind, but couldn't catch the lead boat.

Jules clutched the wheel, the wind whipping through her ponytail. The same frustration etched on the crew's face must be on hers. "We're going to run out of course."

"We'll never catch them this way," Phillipe agreed.

"Alejandro will be satisfied with second place." She thought about the text he'd sent as they headed out.

If we lose the race, we lose. But just being here we've already won.

She'd already won her freedom. She'd lost her family and…

No. Jules needed to focus. "But he deserves a win."

"We can still win," Phillipe said confidently. "But it's going to take the best tack of your life. You up for it?"

She grinned. "Just tell me what to do."

"Not what, when," Phillipe explained. "The rules make it hard to overtake a boat. But if we can tack below and come ahead."

"We'd have luffing rights," she said.

Phillipe winked. "Our helmsman has read the rule book."

Jules nodded. Her hands trembled with excitement and nerves. She wanted to give Alejandro and *La Rueca* the victory.

"The lead boat is tacking on starboard," Phillipe yelled. "Wait for my call."

The crew readied themselves for the final maneuver. They were on port, left of the lead boat. Instead of passing behind their competitor, they were going to tack below them and try to gain the advantage and the lead.

"Now," the tactician ordered.

"Tacking." Julianna turned the wheel. She focused on her job. She knew the other crewmembers were doing theirs, everyone in sync. The wind seemed to be on their side as well.

"Faster," Phillipe yelled.

Jules turned the wheel. Her hands and arms ached

from three days of racing. She ignored the pain, thinking about Alejandro instead. This boat and race meant so much to him. Placing would give him more publicity so he could start turning the island into a sailing-centered tourist spot, but a win would be a huge boost to his boatyard.

He'd helped her. Jules wanted to do the same for him even if he didn't want her the way she wanted him.

She pressed the boat closer to the wind.

Phillipe whistled. "That's it. They're getting our dirty air now."

They edged out in front, taking both the lead and the wind.

"They're falling away," Mike called. "Looks like we can pull this off."

A few minutes later, the prow of *La Rueca* sailed between the buoys marking the finish line. They had done it. They had won the race!

Laughter overflowed along with deafening cheers. Jules wanted to celebrate along with the crew, but the victory was bittersweet.

Yes, she had proven herself. But now that the race was over, she had no idea what would happen. What would she do next?

Exhilaration shot through her. At least she was the one who got to answer that question, not anyone else.

The boat arrived at the marina. Alejandro stood on the dock with champagne bottles. A jubilant smile graced his face. Approval filled his dark eyes.

"Good race." He shook her hand, the pressure warm, secure, making her ache to have him pull her into his embrace. "World class sailing out there, Julianna. You won the race for us."

For you, she wanted to tell him. But seeing him brought a rush of emotion. Tears welled in her eyes. She didn't want to start crying because she was afraid she wouldn't be able to stop.

"Thanks." She forced a smile even though his greeting broke her heart. Not that she expected anything else, but they had won the race. A hug would be…appropriate. "And it's Jules, not Julianna."

"Thank you, Jules," he said.

A member of the yacht club led the crew to a platform surrounded by fans and press. Trophies were handed out. Through it all, Jules kept stealing glances at Alejandro. She forced her attention off him. When a bottle of champagne ended up in her hands, she took a swig.

The crew cheered.

Sam grinned. "Now that's the proper way a princess should drink, mates."

She laughed.

Alejandro pulled her aside. "We need to talk."

Her heart beat as fast as a hummingbird's wings. She followed him to *La Rueca* and climbed aboard. "I'm not going to marry Enrique."

"I know." His mouth twisted with regret. "I'm sorry, Jules. I thought you and Enrique marrying was for the best, but I was fooling myself. I'm miserable without you. I thought I had to rely only on myself.

But I needed you to sail the boat. And then I realized I need you in my life. I love you."

The air rushed from her lungs. "You do?"

"Yes. I do." His tender gaze caressed her face. "I love everything about you. From the way you drive a sailboat to the way you kiss me until I can't think straight. You can go from haughty royal to sweet young thing in about three seconds flat. That made it hard to know the real Julianna or Jules, but I realize she's all of you. And that's okay."

Jules stared up at him. "I'm sorry for what I said to you. I was hurt. Angry. Wrong."

"It's okay now." He squeezed her hand. "I'm here for you. I'll take care of you. I can be a prince if that's what you want. Though you'll never be a queen."

Joy flowed through her, filling up every space inside her. She touched his cheek. "I don't care about being a queen. I don't need you to be a prince. I love you, Alejandro. That's all that matters. But we'll have to take care of each other. Equally. I wouldn't have it any other way."

"Fine by me, Princess." He brushed his lips across hers. "You've already rescued me from being alone, from believing I was the black sheep who had to prove himself, from avoiding my problems with my family and running away from being a prince."

"We rescued each other."

"And we'll continue to do so." Alejandro dropped down on one knee. "I love you, Jules. There's no other woman I'd rather spend the rest of my life with. Will you do me the honor of being my wife?"

"Yes." She pulled him up and kissed him hard on the lips. "A hundred times, yes."

"I want you to pick out a ring you like." He pulled something out of his pocket. A thin piece of line knotted into a ring. "I hope this will do in the meantime."

Tears of love crested her lashes. "It'll do fine."

She'd been wrong. So very wrong.

Alejandro hadn't been selfish. He'd been afraid. But he was still the same dashing hero from her midnight sailing adventure. And she knew from the bottom of her heart, totally devoted to her. Love overflowed as he placed the handmade ring on her finger. A perfect fit.

Her heart sighed. "I'm ready to sail off into the sunset."

"Not yet," he said.

She looked up at him. "I thought..."

"I'm going to marry you, but first I want you to take some time to live your own life. To be on your own before we settle down. Maybe six months to a year. I want you to experience the freedom you've longed for. Travel, sail, whatever you want."

"I want to be with you."

"I want to be with you, but this is too important." He kissed each of her fingers. "Don't worry. I'm not about to let you have all that fun without me. Some things we'll do together. Others you'll do on your own. But know I'll be here to support, love and marry you when it's time."

"I'm counting the days."

"I'll have a real ring for you by then."

She stared at the rope on her finger and smiled up at him. "This ring is real. Like your kisses. Speaking of which…"

He lowered his mouth toward her. "I thought you'd never ask."

EPILOGUE

One year later...

STANDING ON THE deck of the eighty-five-foot sailboat, Jules listened to the wind against the sails. The sun shone high in the blue sky. The oiled teak gleamed. The old-fashioned schooner was something out of a dream or a pirate movie.

Contentment flowed through her. She'd spent the last year chasing her dreams. She'd sailed in numerous races, including winning a prestigious offshore race as part of an all-women's crew. She'd traveled and worked on women's rights issues. All the while Alejandro was there supporting, encouraging and waiting.

But this was the one dream she wanted to make come true.

She couldn't imagine a better place to get married. No heads of state, no strangers, no media in attendance. Only friends and family. Her father, stepmother and four brothers were here as well as Alejandro's father, mother and brother. Not quite a happy family, but Jules hoped in time differences could be...forgotten.

Alejandro squeezed her hand. He stared at her as though she were the sun and his world revolved around her. She felt the same way about him.

"I pronounce you husband and wife." The ship's captain smiled. "You may kiss the bride."

Alejandro's lips pressed against hers, making her feel cherished and loved. Jules kissed him back with her heart and her soul. She wanted him to know how much he meant to her.

Those in attendance clapped and cheered.

"I feel like I'm dreaming," she whispered.

"Wake up, Princess." He brushed his lips across hers. "Your dreams are coming true."

"A happily ever after, too?"

"Nothing less will do." Alejandro ran his finger along her jawline. The caress sent tingles shooting through her. "But we have to do one thing first."

Anticipation buzzed through her. "What?"

"Sail off into the sunset."

Jules's heart overflowed with love. "Sounds perfect."

"Just like you."

"I'm not perfect."

His smile crinkled the corners of his eyes. "Then you're the perfect not-so-perfect princess for me."

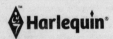